PRAISE FOR *DEAR VIRGINIA, WAIT FOR ME*

"Full of wit, charm, and its fair share of everything bagels, Marcia Butler's moving book manages to be a warm and generous New York novel while grappling with the ghosts of childhood trauma, lost literary heroes, and societal definitions of 'madness.' Her protagonist believes she's being guided by the voice of Virginia Woolf, but it is Butler's voice — comforting and astute, alive to the music of kindness as well as betrayal — that holds you to the end."

— JONATHAN LEE, author of *High Dive* and *The Great Mistake*

"What does it mean to hear voices? *Dear Virginia, Wait for Me* is an original, poignant, and, yes, playful novel that deals with mental health, hidden supports, and the joys of love and abiding friendship. A vibrant book full of charms and surprises."

— JOAN SILBER, author of *Secrets of Happiness* and *Improvement*

"Sometimes, all I want is to be immersed in a world in which the heroine embraces her own quirky brilliance while learning to accept help and love, and, in doing so, redefines family as a way of finding home. Enter Marcia Butler's *Dear Virginia, Wait For Me*, a compelling, sweet, surprising novel with the unworldly and wise Peppa Ryan as its beating heart. I read it in just two sittings, rushing to know how it ends but wishing it would just keep going."

— LORI OSTLUND, author of *Are You Happy?* and *After the Parade*

"As a book populated by those you would gladly share any given evening with, this story would happily grace the time spent. Protagonist Peppa Ryan finds friendship in a way she never could have planned, or even imagined. Better yet, as someone who has never been truly heard, she listens to an inner voice both known and mysterious, and it becomes the key to her very survival. This wonderful novel has changed how, who and what I listen to. May it be that book for you."

— GIL GROSS, broadcast journalist, CBS News

T0348935

"Cinematic and evocative, *Dear Virginia, Wait For Me* explores the serendipity in unexpected, life-altering friendships. With empathy and wit, Marcia Butler introduces us to characters that are simultaneously quirky and relatable, and an expansive New York City ripe with opportunity. Butler's page-turning prose compels us to explore the power of humor and hope in the face of despair."

— KEREN BLANKFELD, author of *Lovers in Auschwitz*

"Enchanting and evocative; every young woman who has struggled to find her true voice in a changing world will see herself in Peppa Ryan."

— JESSICA HANDLER, author of *The Magnetic Girl*

PRAISE FOR *PICKLE'S PROGRESS*

"The four main characters in *Pickle's Progress* seem more alive than most of the people we know in real life because their fears and desires are so nakedly expressed."

— RICHARD RUSSO

"In this study of how childhood experiences shape perception, and how deception keeps people caged, Butler shows that nothing need be set in stone."

— *KIRKUS REVIEWS*

PRAISE FOR *OSLO, MAINE*

"An engaging, wonderfully nuanced novel."

— *NEW YORK JOURNAL OF BOOKS*

"For all their furtiveness, the flawed but deeply relatable characters exude an authentic sense of humanity, making this a sure-fire recommendation for Fredrik Backman fans."

— *BOOKLIST*

"Butler writes beautifully and with depth, each character mined for internal gems."

— *SHELF AWARENESS*

ALSO BY MARCIA BUTLER

The Skin Above My Knee

Pickle's Progress

Oslo, Maine

DEAR VIRGINIA, WAIT FOR ME

WAIT FOR ME

A NOVEL

MARCIA BUTLER

central
avenue

2025

Published by Central Avenue Publishing, an imprint of Central Avenue Marketing Ltd.
www.centralavenuepublishing.com

The epigraph is taken from Virginia Woolf's suicide note.
Quotes by Virginia Woolf from *A Writer's Diary* by Virginia Woolf. Copyright © 1954,
1953 by Leonard Woolf, Copyright renewed 1982, 1981 by Quentin
Bell and Angelica Garnett. Used by permission of HarperCollins Publishers.

Published in Canada
Printed in United States of America

1. FICTION/Coming of Age   2. FICTION/Historical

DEAR VIRGINIA, WAIT FOR ME: A NOVEL

Trade Paper: 978-1-77168-408-8
Ebook: 978-1-77168-409-5

1 3 5 7 9 10 8 6 4 2

Dedicated to, and in memory of,
Dr. Howard Welsh,
who helped so many who suffered.

I feel certain I am mad again.

I feel we can't go through another of those terrible times.

And I shan't recover this time.

I begin to hear voices, and I can't concentrate.

—Virginia Woolf

DEAR VIRGINIA, WAIT FOR ME

SOMEBODY WILL MARRY YOU

PEPPA RYAN SWIVELED AROUND FOR THE THIRD TIME, LOOKING FOR something, anything, familiar. She'd stood at this exact intersection just two weeks before, but now it seemed a bewildering mishmash of commercial real estate, bus exhaust, and people. To her left, a couple of geezers sidestepped an overflowing garbage can in front of a packed Off Track Betting Parlor. To her right, a Chinese laundry gave off a faint odor of perc, and next to it, a deli specializing in everything bagels added a strong layer of yeast. The Family Dollar store, already open, and a Chase Bank, still closed, stood directly across the street. But Peppa remembered none of this. To make matters worse, she was sleep-deprived and anxious, and this combination always produced the uncomfortable sensation of a need for food, at odds with her ongoing resolve to avoid it.

She looked across the street and spied a Queens-bound bus approaching. Now it occurred to her that she really could ditch all of this, an idea she'd been toying with throughout a night of fitful sleep and then the pre-dawn bus ride to Brooklyn. She could race across the street, catch the return bus, and go back home. Become an official no-show. Anyway, what could they do to her? But then she smelled falafels and suddenly remembered the halal cart that had been parked near the building she was currently looking for. She followed her nose and rounded a corner. There was the food cart with an impressive cluster of customers already lined up, despite the early morning hour. And just across the street, she saw the circles stacked horizontally across the façade of the Flatbush Avenue subway, including the red one with the number three in white. Peppa decided this was a good sign.

She slid her new monthly MetroCard through the turnstile and skittered down multiple stairways toward the train that would eventually deposit her in the Wall Street area of Manhattan. Just as she hit the platform, the number three slowed into the station. With dozens ahead of her, Peppa decided to go for it and shouldered her way through, garnering more than a few daggered looks.

"Sure, honey. Whatever you want," one disgruntled man muttered, his arm sweeping a grand gesture toward the train door. Peppa skulked ahead of him and stepped into the car. She'd already endured the almost hour-long bus ride from Sandy Point, Queens, so the timing of the subway was something of a miracle. Yes, part of that lucky sign. And really, if she was actually going to go through with this job thing, arriving late was not an option.

As the train gained speed, she motioned to the sarcastic man, indicating they should switch places. Her idea was to give them both more room, but he didn't seem to appreciate, or even understand, her intention.

"Sure, sweety. Take *aaaall* the space you need."

Once they swapped, she grabbed hold of an overhead pole and scanned the packed train. Some sipped coffee while reading the paper. A few nodded off. One woman wept quietly. But the majority stared into space, looking anywhere but directly into another's face. Peppa thought about this—all these people squished within an inch of one another yet behaving as if they were completely alone. It struck her as a peculiar example of mass delusion. Actually, kind of a joke, and she couldn't help but chuckle out loud, which prompted the man to look up from the *New York Post* he'd buried his nose in.

"You think this is *funny*?"

She shrugged and pursed her lips, determined not to respond. But when she considered the approaching day and all that it portended, the guy had a point. Nothing at all was funny. In fact, this day, of all days, felt as treacherous as walking down a heavy wooden plank suspended off the tip of a flimsy canoe in the middle of a faraway ocean. Peppa was about to plunge into day number one of her very first job.

You will, in all likelihood, do well.

Oh, thank goodness, Peppa thought. There it was: the voice. It had been with her for most of her life, piping up with encouragement at moments when she was fearful, nudging when she doubted herself. She imagined its source as a middle-aged woman with long hair fashioned into a bun at the nape of her neck. A thin nose and slightly sad eyes. Very kind, yet at times quite insistent. Just like a good and true best friend would be. And Peppa wanted to believe that, yes, it was possible that she'd do well.

Now she sensed the weird guy giving her a once-over, so Peppa looked down at the sensible shoes she'd purchased over the weekend. They were meant for comfort, but as with all new shoes, blisters at both heels had already gotten a solid hold. And it was hot in the packed car. She shifted her weight, felt her thighs rub against each other and regretted wearing the formfitting blouse and pencil skirt she'd laid out the previous night. Why hadn't she worn those pantaloon trousers with the elastic waistband her mom had insisted were a more forgiving option? Peppa unbuttoned her wool coat to let in some air and found that her blouse, moist with perspiration, was adhered to the skin below her bra. A rivulet of sweat escaped from her hairline and did a swan dive off an eyelash. She wiped the moisture away and managed to drag some mascara along for the swim. Then she noticed her fingers. Blood in various states of coagulation circled eight out of ten cuticles. When had *that* happened? Suddenly the conductor braked hard and everyone, whether sitting or standing, canted in one direction. Peppa, once again, found herself much too close to the weirdo. He jerked his head back and to the side. Maybe her breath had gone south too. But offending him or any of the other human sardines packed into this speeding tin can was not her biggest concern. It was her new boss Peppa meant to impress, an intention that was now in serious doubt.

They'd finally met at the last of four interviews that had been held over a couple of weeks. The first thing that stood out was his speech. Precisely executed, he had a distinct non-accent, similar to a newscaster. But when he asked if she needed to visit the "loo," Peppa knew he'd spent at least some time in the UK. The other remarkable feature was his outfit. He'd worn a three-piece suit so deeply blue it read as black, except when a particular light caught the fabric weave. And underneath, a lavender shirt with intricate triple stitching around the collar and cuffs. Below the hem of his pant legs, tasseled suede loafers poked out, looking as if they'd never said hello to a pavement in their life. Then, on his right hand, third finger, a thick gold band gripped a red stone. A class ring from some first-rate university, no doubt, though she'd not been able to make out the curlicue lettering. And he was very handsome, with wiry black hair that had been sculpted with enough product to defy hurricane-force winds. She then noticed a tiny dot of blood on the edge of one nostril. To snip nose hairs so close as to draw blood was a level of fussiness Peppa couldn't relate to. She'd grown up around cops and firefighters and those who, like her father, worked in some aspect of the construction trades. Most were hardworking, a few harder drinking.

But they certainly hadn't the time or inclination to consider, much less organize, the insides of their noses. So with all this, it was no surprise that when he offered her the job at the conclusion of that interview, Peppa had spent the next two weeks fretting about what to wear. And now, as if victim to its own gravity field, her pantyhose was slowly but surely slithering down her hips. She gave up on any decorum and yanked them up with a mighty heave-ho. As the doors opened to the final stop in Brooklyn, the weirdo exited with a final shot:

"Don't worry, honey. *Somebody* will marry you."

A perfectly dreadful excuse for a human.

True enough, Peppa thought.

But his words hurt because Peppa knew the truth of it. She wasn't pretty. A gap between her front teeth measuring about an eighth of an inch never failed to elicit bug eyes. But she brought it on herself, because she couldn't help but smile without hesitation, spontaneous even at her own expense. Then there was her pug nose, her alien-looking eyes, her dimpled chin, and her sharp cheekbones, which typically brought on comments like *She's from another planet* or *Where the hell did all* that *come from* or *She's a one-er, all right.* But a point of pride no one could deny was her hair—long, thick, with endless bounce, and as platinum blonde as her first day on earth. In fact, that very morning, Peppa had taken pains to blow out her hair in a style she imagined took the emphasis off her face. Then, before leaving the house, she'd slipped the crisp one-hundred-dollar bill her dad had given her in case of a disaster, along with a certificate of highest honors from the executive assistant program she'd just graduated from, into her purse. But most importantly, a picture of Virginia Woolf, who Peppa believed, no, *knew,* was the voice that spoke to her.

Dear Virginia, Peppa thought, *send me your courage.*

Her stop finally arrived, and Peppa hustled out. She backed herself against a grimy tiled wall, allowing swarms of people to pass, then trotted up the stairway to emerge into a crisp morning. Again, she felt alien. This was not the New York City she'd been raised in. A few blocks from her house, the beach unfurled for miles to the right and left while the water before her presented a horizon line that went all the way to the Connecticut shore. But here, everything was vertical. Impossibly tall buildings lumbered over thin streets, allowing only a small slice of sunlight to reach the sidewalks. She took tentative steps toward the building she hoped to call *her* building, while dodging people speed-walking against her like firefighters racing to a five-alarm. Others were corralled in clumps on both sides of the entrance doors, smoking. That they all wore a mask of unhappiness added to Peppa's apprehension. But she reminded herself that she'd won a job in a prestigious investment firm, and this was supposed to be a good thing.

Once inside the lobby, she queued up for one of many elevators. The time was just before 8 a.m., and she was surprised by the number of people already waiting. One after the next, each elevator filled to capacity, and it took Peppa twenty minutes to reach her floor. Though her final interview had been conducted here, she couldn't remember which direction to walk. Every hallway looked identical and there were no signs or arrows, as if the building was so famous, well, don't be ridiculous. But she was still quite early, so she looped around a bit, gawking right, left, up, down, like a bumpkin from the backwoods. Then, a ladies' room appeared. She had needed to pee for quite some time, so she pushed in to find a line of women waiting for the occupied stalls. The room reeked, and on instinct Peppa covered her nose with her hand. A pale, rangy woman nodded with a sympathetic smile.

"Some people have no consideration," the woman whispered.

The line was long, so Peppa stepped in front of a mirror above the bank of sinks and removed her coat to assess her outfit—a mess from neck to waistband.

"Just spritz some water on those stains, then use the blow dryer," the same woman directed.

Peppa ran her hand under the faucet, then patted water under her arms and at her bra line. She aimed the blower toward her torso and in less than a minute the sweat evaporated, or at least was now less noticeable.

"Turn around," the woman commanded, then pointed to the wet Rorschach along Peppa's spine.

"Oh, right," Peppa said. She didn't particularly care about a sweat stain she couldn't see and was getting a tad weary of receiving orders from a perfect stranger. But she placated the woman again, aiming the hot air at her back. Now the stalls had mostly emptied out, so the woman took her turn and peed interminably. Peppa dabbed soap on the mascara smears beneath both eyes, then rubbed vigorously with a paper towel. When the woman reappeared, she looked at Peppa as if considering a purchase.

"Great hair."

Peppa gave up a smile.

"And cool teeth. Lauren Hutton. She's got teeth like yours. Which office do you work at?"

Peppa waited a beat, then slowly assembled the still-unfamiliar words. "Lafferty, Beck and Stern."

"Me too," the woman said, stifling a yawn. She leaned against a wall and cocked her head with curiosity. "Who's your boss?"

"Ivan Scherbo. It's my first day."

"Huh. You must be *very* good. He interviewed close to thirty people." The woman leaned over the sink and drank water from her hand. "He's compulsive. Things have to be perfect," she warned between gulps. "Quite a taskmaster, I've heard."

A weak laugh was all Peppa could summon, then she glanced at her watch. "God, it's almost half eight. Excuse me."

She chose the farthest stall, hoping to gain psychic distance from the woman. Plus, she'd been standing among hundreds of people since exiting the bus from Queens, so it was a relief to finally be able to sit down in privacy, even if on a toilet. She slung her purse and coat on the door hook and shimmied the pantyhose down her legs, squishing them around her ankles. Now it occurred to her that she'd likely spend the day pulling them up every fifteen minutes, so she slid off her shoes, gathered the pantyhose into a wad, and stuffed them into the sanitary napkin can. Then she noticed that the blisters on her heels had popped. She palmed some spit, patted it into the sore wounds, then blotted the whole mess with toilet paper.

"Where're you from?"

The woman chose to ask this question while Peppa was midstream. Her bladder seized. Was it too much to ask, to have a pee in peace? She quickly finished up and exited the stall.

"Here. The city," she answered. "But my parents are from Ireland."

"I *thought* so. There was one phrase I detected. But it's barely noticeable. I'm Lorraine, by the way."

"Penelope Ryan. I'm called Peppa."

"*Peppa*? Okaaaay," Lorraine said, as if her nickname would be an ongoing hardship.

They walked to the office together, which was awkward enough. But when she asked the receptionist where her desk was, to Peppa's dismay, Lorraine's workstation partition happened to be common with hers. If they both stood up at their desks, they'd face each other.

"You might want to wear layers tomorrow," Lorraine advised. "They keep the office like a meat locker. Some nonsense about productivity. I have an extra sweater if you need one."

Peppa shook her head and made herself look busy. Furrowing her brow with fake concentration, she opened and closed all the desk drawers, then fussed over adjusting her chair to a height that suited her. Now she wiggled the lumbar lever endlessly. All in the hope that Lorraine would get the hint. But she just kept nodding and shaking her head as if supervising.

"I'm sorry, Lorraine, but it's my first day and all. Do you mind if I have some privacy?"

"The last one didn't make it past the first day. Come to think of it, she got canned before noon," Lorraine quipped before dipping behind the partition.

Peppa slumped in her seat, laid her head on the desk, and tried not to cry. She'd never worked in a big-time office environment before and wondered if Lorraine was actually trying to sabotage her. And now she couldn't help but recap all her many missteps since the moment she woke that morning. Wearing pantyhose being the worst, because now she saw that the backs of her clodhopping shoes had dug into her heels even more, causing them to ooze blood. She kicked them off and grabbed some loose tissues from her purse, folding them into rectangles. Then she placed the makeshift bandages across her heels and put her shoes back on. If she was lucky, this would hold for maybe an hour. If she didn't have to walk.

But forget about walking anywhere. What was she even supposed to be *doing*? Her boss had been in a hurry the day of her final interview. After a short chat he simply exclaimed, *You're hired!* and raced out the door. HR followed up with her contract and start date, of course, but it wasn't until this very second that Peppa realized she was unclear as to what her job actually entailed. Just like the *last one* Lorraine had mentioned, Peppa was doomed to be fired, and likely before the hour was up.

One often neglects what I consider the most useful of the senses. To Listen.

Now Peppa heard the collective computer keystrokes throughout the office. Even Lorraine was banging away, though Peppa noted that she could easily type twice Lorraine's speed. But aside from momentary gloating, she now realized that what Virginia probably meant, because this was the modern world after all, was that she should power up her computer. And the next logical move would be to open her email account. But then, *oh God*. Peppa had already received no less than ten messages from her boss, the first having been sent at 5 a.m. Was she actually expected to access emails before daybreak? And how would she even do that, other than leaving her house at three in the morning in order to arrive at five. This was not going well.

She swiveled around. The office appeared to be in major panic mode—everyone hunched over their desks, peering at screens, talking in frantic whispers into phones. Wearing oversized sweaters and scarfs, a few sporting mittens with the fingers cut off. Clearly freezing, per Lorraine. But Peppa wasn't the least bit cold, which she took as a bad sign that she didn't belong in this office or even on the island of Manhattan. In any case, it was obvious that the entire staff *had* arrived at an ungodly hour—something everyone understood to be protocol for all Wall Street investment firms. Except her. And what was the *last one* doing now? Had she gotten a new job? Maybe she lived with her parents like Peppa did, so getting fired wasn't a complete hardship. Still . . . the *last one* . . . poor thing. All these thoughts sifted through Peppa's mind like a cascade of predestined disasters, pretty much assuring her dismissal within the hour. This was exhausting.

The very best use of time — really, the dearest thing — is to read.
Oh Virginia, Peppa thought, *what an idiot I am.*

A quick perusal of the 5 a.m. emails revealed them to be the standard job protocols she'd already memorized from her contract. She was so relieved she laughed out loud.

"What's so funny?" Lorraine asked from the other side of the partition.

"Oh . . . nothing. Nothing is funny."

The most recent email had been sent when Peppa was manhandling her chair. It listed bullet points about the client on tap for the morning, with his dossier attached. She now remembered her boss's one and only admonition during the final interview: she was to individually acknowledge every email, even if there was nothing in particular to address. The rule had made her smile because she also disliked it when com-

8

munications floated in space, leaving the sender to wonder if it had even been seen, much less read. Buoyed by the thought that she and her boss might be in sync, at least on the belief that hostility was embedded in the act of unacknowledged emails, she enthusiastically signed off on each one.

"CONFIRMED—PR."

Then, as if he'd been waiting for her to do just that, a response immediately flew back. "COME ON IN."

Oh no. Was he mocking her with the caps? She hadn't meant to shout.

When she entered his office, Peppa was blinded by what seemed to be a spotlight aimed directly into her eyes. But after blinking a few times, her vision adjusted, and she saw that it was just the fierce morning sun saturating floor-to-ceiling windows. Quickly scanning that side of the room, she noticed the colors on the walls and furniture were variations of creams and beiges, which made the space appear larger than the smallish room it was. She spied packets of peanuts and other nibble foods artfully stacked next to water bottles on a credenza. Her stomach rumbled, and she realized how terribly hungry she was. Her mom had left a stack of pancakes from the previous morning in the microwave to be reheated for breakfast, but she'd been much too nervous to eat and left the house having downed only a cup of tea. Peppa felt an urge to snag some peanuts then and there but didn't dare because when she turned around, she discovered her boss sitting in the center of the sofa with an open laptop on his knees. He wore a light beige suit, which appeared to be the exact same color as the sofa fabric, and black high-top sneakers that disappeared into the dark plaid of the carpet. His hair was parted in the opposite direction from the way she remembered it from two weeks before.

He closed the laptop and smiled. She smiled back, but closed-lipped, mindful not to expose the embarrassing gap between her front teeth.

"Welcome, Ms. Ryan. Very good to see you. Make yourself comfortable and we'll have a wee chat."

There it was again. That British Isles thing. He gestured for her to sit in one of two club chairs opposite the sofa.

"So," he began. "Just to state the obvious, I was very pleased with your entire interview process. Intuition and cognition tests landed you in the top point-five percentile. Your writing sample read like the prose of early twentieth-century British novelists. What was it called—the Bloomsbury Group? Like . . . Virginia Woolf."

"Yes!" she blurted out. "I mean . . . I do admire Woolf. Very much."

He raised his left eyebrow and gave her a tight nod. "Other skills, such as fluency with multiple software systems, are simply first rate. And your typing is faster than anyone we've ever tested. This is all to say that I feel fortunate you applied for the job. I've had a challenging time landing the right person." He paused here and leaned forward, looking as if about to say something she'd reminisce about for years to come, in the category of: *I'll never forget what my first boss said on my first day of work. It literally changed my life!*

"Ms. Ryan, I believe you're the *full* package."

An unfortunate choice of words. Peppa squirmed in her seat, aware of her waistband pressing into her stomach flesh. Of course, she knew his gaffe was unintended. But the praise about her skills caused a trickier sort of discomfort. It was true that she could perform tons of office/businesslike things with ease, and that she read voraciously. In short, she was whip smart. And how nice that he'd gleaned all of that. The thing was . . . well . . . there were a bunch of things. Such as the fact that Peppa had a photographic memory for anything written on a page. A careful once-over embedded a picture in her mind that she could then reconjure precisely. So she'd never needed to memorize or study. Peppa simply *saw*. Then the dexterity thing, which apparently had just won her *Miss NYC Fastest Typist of November 2000*. This trait first expressed itself in the enormous Lego kingdoms she'd assembled as a young girl. She could imagine complex buildings in her head, then construct them without a second of hesitation, all within the span of just an hour or two. When that became a bore, she decided to assemble them by touch only, while blindfolded. Which is how her fingers could do many things without relying on eyesight. Like typing. So, receiving praise for doing things that required almost no effort had always felt like cheating. She would have much preferred to have a slim body, and she'd settle for a reasonably decent-looking face.

Just as she was about to say *thank you*, another response occurred to Peppa. If she were truly as smart as people seemed to think—or simply a realist—she'd leave immediately and ride the subway underwater to Brooklyn and then the bus over the bridge to Sandy Point. She'd run the many blocks to her house. Shut the front door while preventing the latch from clicking, so her mom wouldn't hear her. Slip off her shoes, letting the bloody bandages fall off her heels, and pad up the stairs. Crawl into bed. Cry really hard. Swallow two of her mom's tranquilizer pills that she'd pilfer on occasion and hide behind Virginia's *Orlando,* which she'd been meaning to read for the longest time. Then, finally, sleep in an anesthesia blackout. Eventually, she'd wake to her parents arguing outside her door about the fact that she'd been asleep for over twenty-four hours. Only then would she listen to the voicemail her boss would surely have left, asking why she'd walked out. If there was anything he'd done wrong. And would she consider returning. Because, he'd say, everything would be okay. But nothing, nothing at all, had ever been okay. And now, a tear was about to fall from Peppa's left lower eyelash, and she very much hoped her boss wouldn't notice.

Regardless of whatever else is on one's mind, a courteous response is usually the wisest course of action.

At Virginia's prompt, she managed to squawk out, "Thank you, Mr. Scherbo."

"I see I've embarrassed you. Forgive me."

He smiled broadly, and Peppa was heartened to see that his teeth were discolored and kind of crooked. At least they had imperfect teeth in common. She felt slightly less awful.

"Well, maybe a little. I'm . . . I'm just super nervous."

"I can understand that. But I simply wanted to bring your talents out into the open, so to speak. Everyone works to their best capacity when their value is acknowledged."

No one had ever referred to her as having *value* before. "I guess . . ."

"That's usually the way it works. Don't you think?"

Before she could answer, Peppa's stomach released an extended and very loud howl. Her hand floated to her mouth to suppress a giggle. He broke into laughter and pointed to the stockpile.

"Want some kibbles and bits?" he asked, pointing to the human Meow Mix.

"I could do with some," she answered.

"Help yourself. And grab a water for me while you're at it."

Emboldened, she fetched multiple bags and water bottles from the credenza, then divided the spoils between them on the coffee table. They spent a few minutes palming nuts into their mouths and chugging water straight from the bottle. When they finished, he brushed his hands free of salt, adjusted his cuffs, and pinched his bow tie. Then, planting an elbow on the arm of the sofa, he propped a closed fist under his chin and peered at her. Lord, now what. More compliments she hadn't earned? More likely, he'd just realized she was the *wrong* package and was about to give her the sack. Then she'd become the new *last one*. And well deserved, because what was she even *doing*? Her boss had eaten one package of nuts and was still sipping his first bottle of water. She, on the other hand, had gobbled sack after sack of peanuts, candied raisins, and miniature Fig Newtons while slugging back *two* waters. And she'd just finished wiping her mouth with the back of her hand. What a feral beast she was! But he said nothing and just placed some papers on top of the empty foil wrappers scattered across the coffee table. Probably a termination document. Now he folded his arms across his chest. *Here we go*, Peppa thought. *I'm toast.* Because really, she was nothing more than an average Queens girl with the manners of a starved mongrel.

"These are your aptitude tests. You can look at them if you want. But I'm curious about something. They show a strong intuition for business practices, but you didn't list any job experience. In fact, you almost didn't make the résumé cut because of that. Luckily, somebody in HR noticed you'd graduated from that ad-assist program with exceptionally high marks and dragged you back onto the potentials list. To be honest, I was so pleased when we met at your interview it slipped my mind to ask. But you must have at least some work experience."

"My parents own a small business. I've helped out," she offered quietly.

"Interesting. What sort of business?"

"Construction."

"That's pretty broad. Do they specialize?"

"Homes. Apartments. Fix-ups. Things like that."

"And what did you do?"

"Everything." The word fell out of her mouth and she felt like a bragger. "Except the labor, of course."

He laughed. "Yes, I'd expect not. Well. That's it then. Now, a bit about our clients. They can be annoying. A few are irrational. And I'm sure you know this, but money is a lot like love. People want more and more of both. But neither makes anyone truly happy, at least not in the way we imagine. That's a metaphor you'll hear me repeat ad nauseam."

The scent of money? The vagaries of love? Did he really think she knew about such things? Well, aside from her third-rate appearance, how could he know that she came from a bottom-of-the-pile, working-class family.

He glanced at his watch. "First one arrives in thirty minutes."

"Yes, yes. I downloaded his file."

"Excellent. He's not a bad sort. Just . . . stiff. These meetings last anywhere from one to two hours. You'll need to behave as if you're the proverbial fly on the wall. In fact, it's best if the client forgets you're even in the room. You're to take verbatim notes on the entire conversation, including any chitchat you might think has nothing to do with my job or their money. The firm is particular about this because I don't record as many managers do. So, your accuracy is crucial."

"I understand," Peppa said, nodding vigorously.

"Also, you should know that my clients are . . . well, let's just say they're kind of spoiled. They don't like to wait for much of anything. So, I'd like you to greet them at the elevator. Walk them directly into the office. Bypass the receptionist entirely, even if she tries to flag you down. They feel more important this way."

"But how will I know? I mean . . . when they're in the elevator."

"Get to the elevator bank ten minutes before their appointment and wait. Their pictures are part of the portfolio. Though, come to think of it, most are at least thirty years older and thirty pounds heavier. But I'm sure you'll be able to make the adjustment. Are we clear?"

"Crystal," she said with a kind of steely Tom Cruise non-inflection.

He did a double take and laughed. Peppa hadn't expected him to get the reference.

"Jack Nicholson," he murmured. "That was some tour de force performance. '*You want me on your wall,*'" he growled. "Okay, Ms. Ryan, scoot. We've got a full morning ahead of us."

As he opened his laptop and began typing, Peppa lingered at the door, observing him and wondering what kind of person her boss really was. He seemed a mix of formal and familiar, all at once. But in spite of this contradiction, she knew instinctively that he wasn't out to trip her up. In fact, nothing at all about him seemed devious. "Mr. Scherbo?"

"Hmmm?" he said without looking up.

"Call me Peppa."

He stared into her eyes for several seconds, then smiled. "Makes sense. I'm Ivan."

As soon as Peppa returned to her desk, Lorraine popped up with a pink fleece blanket draped around her shoulders.

"How'd it go?" she asked while jabbing a chopstick at her scalp in an attempt to secure a haystack at the top of her head.

"Well, he didn't fire me."

"The last one couldn't keep up with the transcription—"

"Wait a second." Peppa needed to halt another installment of *the tragic life of the last one.* "If that was the reason she was fired, all I can say is at my final interview he tested me by reading from the *Wall Street Journal* as fast as he could. He seemed pleased. Anyway, he's nice. I mean, we actually laughed a little."

"*Really?*"

"It's true."

"That's unbelievable!" Lorraine squinted. "Well. There's one more thing I need to warn you about."

"What?"

"Y2K."

"What about it?"

"Watch your computer for glitchy bugs."

"Wasn't that debunked months ago? I mean, it's November—ten months in. And nothing's happened."

"That's what they want you to *think.*"

"They?"

"You know, the people—"

Tardiness is the equivalent of a temporary death.

The client! Peppa raced down the hallway, leaving Lorraine to *the people.* Having exited the office with no clue of the correct way, she stopped an older woman and begged her to lead her to the elevators.

"This building is like a maze. C'mon," the woman said, pulling Peppa by the arm.

They rounded what seemed like half a dozen corners. Then, there was the client, gesticulating with one hand while snarling the word *never* over and over into his phone. He did appear much older than his portfolio picture, as Ivan had warned, but still cut a slim figure. His hair, close-cropped in military fashion, looked as white as

14

overly bleached flour. And his face was lined and deeply bronzed. He slapped his flip phone closed after assuring whoever he was talking to that there were enough doggie treats in the pantry for the next month. Peppa approached and initiated introductions, during which he gave her the expected up and down, pausing to feast his eyes on her breasts before returning to her face. Then he shrugged as if all hope was lost and set off toward the office. No matter how Peppa tried to keep pace, he quickened his gait accordingly. The man didn't want to be seen with her.

When they arrived at Ivan's office, Peppa was somewhat distressed by his absence. But the man found it *egregious*, announcing that he hated waiting for *anyone*. He waved off her suggestion of a coffee, so it seemed the only thing left to do was stand side by side at the windows and stare at the Statue of Liberty.

"What a view!" the man declared, managing to pull himself out of his bratty mood. "The Trade Towers are the only legitimate place to conduct business. Adds a great deal of class to what can be a dirty little topic."

"You mean money?"

"Yes, girlie. The subject in this office would be money."

Where was *Ivan*? And how was she supposed to make nice with this snarky man? Then she remembered catching a glimpse of the sports section while riding the bus. Peppa didn't know any man who didn't, at least to some degree, keep tabs.

"How about those Yankees? Another World Series under their belts," she said, punctuating with a thumbs-up to signal she was an enthusiast, though she wasn't at all.

"I'm a Red Sox fan, dear," he replied with enough pity for the great unwashed.

"Oh. How did they do this season?"

"Obviously, they didn't make the playoffs."

Peppa decided she'd better switch to another sport. "My dad likes the European soccer."

"*Fasc*inating."

"I follow it too. Exciting. Riveting, actually. Nonstop action. Baseball is so slow. Seems like there's a lot of waiting around."

"It's a *nuanced* sport," he oozed like a bored educator.

"How so?"

The man moved closer to the window, watching a news helicopter dip down between the Towers, and began to explain everything to the view. "The strategies are complex. Each play is based on stats, and there's a lot of memorization involved. Particularly for the pitcher and the catcher. So, appreciating the game requires a good amount of patience." Now he turned and looked directly at her. "And a better than average intelligence."

"Oh. I get it."

"Do you?"

"Sure. You're saying that people who don't appreciate baseball are kind of dumb."

The man nodded sagely. "That about sums it up, girlie."

"Then why do the fans get so drunk? I mean, they act like a bunch of complete fools—" What in God's name was she *doing*? This guy was a client. He'd complain. She'd get fired. Just like the *last one*. And where the hell was Ivan?

When enduring extraordinary circumstances, you must control yourself, or, if possible, leave the vicinity.

Peppa thought, *Thank you, Virginia*.

She mumbled an *excuse me*, ran to the door, and stuck her head out just in time to see Ivan rounding the corner at a trot. He scooted past her, grabbed the man's hand, and pulled him toward the sofa, smothering him with profuse apologies. Like a miracle, the man melted into Ivan's aura, and it felt like she'd been forgiven. Or more likely, forgotten. Her chair, for purposes of transcribing, had been positioned behind them, though she could still see Ivan's face. Peppa placed the laptop on her thighs, felt for the keyboard, and closed her eyes.

They began with icebreakers. How they both detested the current Jeff Koons exhibit, and how annoying it was that the employees at Citarella had been on strike for a fourth week. Peppa had never heard of Jeff, and in what universe could you be annoyed, even a little, by a strike? Her dad always insisted that striking was the working man's only real tool of power. Then, just as Ivan broached the topic of his portfolio, the man blurted out that his life was in an *unbearable* shambles due to a mistress he was supporting with a huge monthly income. Peppa opened her eyes at this unexpected disclosure just in time to see Ivan raise his left eyebrow. It seemed the man was familiar with the eyebrow's power because he immediately and vigorously assured Ivan that floating her was all fine. And well and good. Not a problem. *Really*. No, the shamble was that the mistress was now insisting that he excise the wife of forty years, his four grown kids, and his eleven grandbabies, out of his will. And insert her. Up went the eyebrow again. Now the man seemed desperate for the eyebrow to understand him—that is, get back in line with the other one. So, he recounted both sides of the "never" phone call. She was blackmailing him with threats of withholding certain bedroom antics. Something to do with body contortions. Something to do with the number 69, a numeral Peppa had always quite liked because of its visual symmetry, now forever debased it seemed, though she didn't know precisely how.

Peppa typed along without a hiccup, feeling disgusted that this guy was using Ivan like a back-alley shrink. But as Ivan began to probe the man for more details, she heard the tone and pitch of his voice change. Soothing, and lilting up and down as the emphasis required. And his skill: deftly poking holes in the man's absurd belief that he had no other choice but to obey the mistress. At the end of the two-hour meeting, the man agreed that the entire family should stay in the will and the mistress would continue to live well enough. That is, if he had the guts to turn the tables and threaten to give her the boot, and with no money, if she didn't satisfy the number 69.

Dear Virginia, Peppa thought, *the human race is doomed.*

As Peppa escorted the man back to the elevator, he was now in such a good mood that he actually attempted conversation. Sports again. Some blather about being a scratch golfer. She didn't buy it. Not only had the guy already admitted to being a cheater in the bedroom, but everybody knew that golf was the only game you could cheat at like crazy because you *kept your own score.* Peppa wondered if the wife, or the mistress, actually believed he hit par 90 percent of the time.

Not five seconds after she returned to her desk, Lorraine foot-scooted her chair around the partition and parked herself. "Here. Put this sweater on," she commanded, dangling something that looked like a limp black cat.

"I'm good. The temperature doesn't bother me."

"It gets colder as the day goes on. Trust me."

Peppa took the sweater and noticed food stains splattered on the front. It reeked of the cockroach spray her dad used in their kitchen to deal with regular infestations, and with little success. "But it smells."

Lorraine buried her nose in the sweater, inhaling and exhaling several times. "I don't smell anything. But how did it go? I mean, what happened in there?"

"We worked. What else would happen?"

"I know he can be tough."

"Not so far."

"Do you want to get a beer and burger after work?"

"Um . . . thanks, but no. I really have to get home tonight. Maybe another time."

Lorraine crab-walked her way back to the other side of the partition. Then, just as Peppa opened her computer to review the transcript, a new message from Ivan arrived. She quickly read through the email and took a deep breath. She looked around the office. The co-workers she'd not even met yet were still buried in other people's money and privilege. She assumed it was like this every day, week after week, month after month. But for Peppa, every single thing in the world was about to change. And now she couldn't help but think of her dad. When the unexpected happened, he'd occasionally make up phrases on the spot that perfectly expressed his surprise. She remembered going with him to a construction site where they found the workers sitting on the floor of a back bedroom with a nice game of poker going. "What in the flickety, flockity, fuckity *hell* is going on?" he'd screamed.

Now Peppa whispered to herself, "What kind of balls, bees, batshit crazy is this?" Because Ivan's email was completely *nuts*.

Dear Virginia, Peppa thought, *is this a dream?*

Dear Peppa,

This email is for your eyes only. With the exception of the top echelon, no one at LBS has knowledge of what I am about to disclose. And forgive me for not being straightforward from the beginning of the interview process. I had to see if you were a "go" before I told you what I really do, what your actual job will be, and how you and I are going to work together. I am what is known as a corporate philanthropist. Most of my time is dedicated to helping companies who develop products or systems that will make a positive impact on third world countries and struggling urban and rural communities. I assess their financials top to bottom and then, if they pass muster, invest on their behalf. LBS acts as a fiduciary umbrella for these efforts. I prefer my work to be anonymous because I don't want to sift through a hundred cold pitches every week. So, I've developed an under-the-radar method of solicitation through select channels and until now have managed to do my work alone. Recently though, I've found I cannot keep up, which is why I've been interviewing for assistants.

The morning clients represent a small slice of my day, and you'll continue transcribing. But the majority of our time will be devoted to the philanthropic work. Your task is to thoroughly investigate the companies that have made a preliminary jump to the top of my stack. They have to be squeaky clean, with no questionable associations and especially no intention of ever going public. I've found that companies quickly lose all moral and ethical backbone when they are beholden to stockholders. Not only will you assess their financial solvency, but also the proposal and mission statement. This will require in-depth research so that you are fully conversant with their product. Finally, after completing this vetting, I'd like your opinion—what you see as strengths, as well as your concerns about potential weak spots. Be specific. Write extravagantly. Provide any and all nuance, even if you think it picky. In short, hold nothing back. Because in essence, Peppa, you will act as my gatekeeper. By now you're likely wondering, why you? Well, I've hired and fired lots of people over the last several months. And while this didn't feel especially good, the process did help me to refine and distill what I truly need in an assistant. Someone who hasn't been over-educated. Or more precisely, someone who hasn't had their imagination and creativity educated *out* of them. Discipline is a must. Bravery, a plus. And in an odd way, someone who I suspect will continue to surprise me. You, Peppa, fit that bill. You're surely wondering how I deduced this, especially after just one morning of work. Based on your fine analytic mind and terrific writing skills, I have a high degree of confidence. But more importantly, what I sensed this morning were your uninhibited instincts, which I believe are an indicator as to how your potential will play out. I am rarely wrong about such things, so I ask that you trust me.

Finally, let me be crystal clear. My wall? It is *our* wall. I consider our work to be a partnership. When you confirm that you've read this email, I'll send you three proposals. Refrain from discussing them with me or even asking any questions. I believe that if you can tolerate the discomfort of not knowing what the hell you're doing—because make no mistake, you *will* feel in over your head— you'll ultimately go much farther and a lot deeper. Complete this work by Friday.

Doing one's work is like taking a breath, and then another.

Yes, yes, Virginia, Peppa thought.

"CONFIRMED—PR."

In less than thirty seconds, another email with the three attachments arrived. The title of one immediately piqued Peppa's interest. "TOILETS." She skimmed the twenty-page document, learning that a fledgling nonprofit sought funding for the production of an experimental toilet that didn't require a water supply and was specifically mandated for remote areas of the southwest Navajo Nation. Peppa was doubtful. No water? Seemed iffy. She knew lots of plumbers through the family business who'd scoff at the very idea. But Ivan must have thought it had merit, because he'd included it in her first batch. Then again, maybe he was testing her by presenting a ludicrous proposition just to see what she'd do with it.

Insecurity and paranoia, regrettable features of the human condition, must be contained at the least, and at an ideal, extinguished.

Peppa thought, *I'll try, Virginia.*

She began on the internet with a deep dive into the history of toilets and sanitation, finding the subject fascinating. The toilet—a contraption most everyone took for granted, was in many ways as life-changing as the printing press. Yet she was shocked to learn that 25 percent of the world's population didn't have toilets or even access to potable water. The decomposition of bodily waste and the metallurgic properties of pipes proved intriguing sidebars she couldn't resist. But after just a few hours, and to her dismay, Peppa discovered that another company was attempting the same thing, but for Bangladesh. Now that a competitor was nipping at their heels, she found herself rooting for the little start-up called Straight Flush.

Throughout the afternoon, Peppa had been so absorbed that when she finally stood up to stretch, she found the entire office empty. A cleaning crew was assembling to begin dusting surfaces and emptying wastebaskets. Lorraine's sweater had been draped over the back of her chair. She smelled it again. It really wasn't that bad—it just needed a wash. She folded it up and placed it on Lorraine's desk, then grabbed her coat and left for home.

OUR GIRL

PEPPA BARRELED THROUGH THE FRONT DOOR OF HER HOUSE AND ENTERED AN empty kitchen. Her parents hadn't waited dinner—their plates were picked clean, a beer stood half finished, chairs sat at careless angles. A tea towel covered the food on her plate. She knew it was chicken because every Monday her mom prepared a Perdue Oven Stuffer. Hot dogs on Tuesday, spaghetti on Wednesday, meatloaf on Thursday. By Friday morning, her mom would announce that her role as domestic slave was basted, poked, charred, done. So, they'd scavenge leftovers and make do with pizza on Saturday. Irish stew, the only food that ever tasted properly seasoned, was the Sunday midday meal. The lineup had never changed.

Peppa peeled back a corner of the towel and pressed her finger into the Monday bird. At least it was still warm. Even so, her parents' absence diminished the excitement she felt about her new job and how surprisingly well the first day had gone. But she couldn't blame them. Supper at 6 p.m. sharp was something her dad insisted on, and she *was* an hour late. Still. Today of all days.

She settled at the table and sliced into the meat. Not too terribly dry. The red potatoes were another story. They'd adhered themselves to a coagulated puddle of chicken fat and Wesson oil. Her mom was tone-deaf to Peppa's frequent pleas for low-calorie preparation. While scraping glop off the spuds, she could hear her parents talking behind the door that led directly into what used to be a greenhouse. Several years back, her mom's scrawny tomato crop had been sacrificed to their expanding construction business. It was now a makeshift office, where they often retreated after dinner to decompress from the day and prepare for the next. Peppa stilled herself, trying to grab bits of conversation, but could make out only soft inflections. And now she imagined them nodding to each other in agreement. Her mom and dad rarely fought about the business, or much else for that matter. But recently they'd argued a lot about Peppa's job-hunting efforts, and well within earshot, as if she were an inconsequential bystander. At first they were convinced she'd never actually go through with *any* job. But once she got the offer and accepted, they downshifted, figuring that when she experienced the drudgery of a daily three-hour round-trip commute, she'd quickly recognize the folly and return to her roots. Work the family business. Caged behind that door. For the rest of her life. Peppa stared at the half-eaten bird and considered its doomed fate. That was how her parents assumed her new job would end up—slaughtered before it even got started. And how pathetic that a dead bird was a metaphor for her future.

Now her dad's voice rose in pitch with a whoop. A few seconds later, they bustled into the kitchen, her dad making a fist-pump as if his daily scratch Lotto ticket had finally paid off.

"We *won* it," he said, grabbing a cold beer from the fridge.

"It's a miracle, that's for sure," her mom said with less enthusiasm.

"The Lotto? We're millionaires!" Peppa couldn't help but joke.

"I wish. Almost as good, though. That Manhattan bid. The one with the massive budget. Remember?" He took a deep swallow, foam grabbing his upper lip.

"Yes, of course," Peppa said, nodding slowly. "This is really good news. It's a huge building. You'll get lots of referrals."

"We'll see. That's the hope, anyway," her mom said.

"Well, I don't see why you wouldn't," she countered.

"Peppa. Eat your dinner," her mom ordered.

She forked a potato into her mouth and chewed slowly, waiting for them to ask the obvious. But her mom turned to the sink to scrape crud off the roasting pan while her dad buried himself in the *Daily News* sports section.

"Nothing about the soccer quarterfinals," he murmured after folding up the paper.

"You'll catch it in the morning edition, I expect," her mom said.

"What happened with that plumbing inspection? Did it get scheduled?"

"Not yet."

"Client's gonna howl something fierce," he predicted.

"The expeditor said the DOB is still backed up from Hurricane Floyd."

"Call the client tomorrow, will you, Patrice? Explain how it's not our fault."

Patrice rubbed damp hands on her apron, then ripped the crossword page from the paper. She read each clue, then printed the word, one after the next. Meanwhile,

Peppa's dad nibbled on the shortbread cookies he swore helped ease his chronic in-digestion. Shortly, he released a few belches, a sign of some relief. Another typical evening. But it wasn't.

There are situations that arise when one has no other choice but to make oneself heard; that is to say, known.

Sure, Virginia, Peppa thought, *but you don't know them.*

Despite her doubts, Peppa decided to try. "Don't you want to know how it went?" she asked quietly. Her dad opened his mouth only to slam it shut when her mom glared at him.

"We're sure it went fine," Patrice said.

Peppa pushed her half-eaten meal to the middle of the table. She felt slightly sick to her stomach and grabbed a cookie.

"Not until you finish your meal," her mom admonished.

Peppa shoved the entire thing in her mouth. "I have to . . . leave . . . at six . . . to-morrow morning," she mumbled between chews and apropos of nothing.

"I read that contract. Says *nine* to *five*," her dad said, jabbing a finger at both numbers.

"My boss is really nice."

"We're sure he is," was all her mom offered before flipping the crossword over to start on the Sudoku.

"Nine to five," he repeated. He began extracting dirt from under his fingernails with the toothpick he always kept in his breast pocket.

"But I have to fit in."

"You fit in there just fine," he said, aiming the toothpick toward the greenhouse-cum-office.

There was no point in challenging him. Because in truth they all knew how bad-ly she was needed at home. Peppa could read complex architectural floor plans and millwork details upside-down and backwards. Probably from a rearview mirror if they ever taught her to drive, something her dad had never found the time to do. And she'd been a stand-in for her mom with pitch-perfect emails since her mid-teens. But Peppa's biggest contribution to the business was analytic. Just recently she'd been able to demonstrate how they lost money accepting jobs below a certain budget. Initially, her dad scoffed because how could that be? A job was a job. Money was money. But

Peppa steered his attention to the X-factor—that time was time. For a few weeks, she clocked every minute of his day including travel, along with the many hours her mom sat at her desk. Then she fed that total into algorithms common to the construction business. And there, at the very bottom of the red column, sat the proof—small projects netted an embarrassingly low income, if any at all. Her dad took the bombshell in silence but had since declined bidding on jobs he now referred to as toilet feeders.

"Anyway, your mother needs to ease up," he continued while stretching his legs. A roach approached his boot, and he perfunctorily squashed it.

Her mom looked up from the puzzle. "Stop pushing me into a coffin, Declan."

"I want grandkids before I tank."

"Do you want her to work in the business or have a baby?"

"She's twenty."

"Will you stop with the non sequiturs?"

"All I'm saying is we were already married at her age. And we both worked." He paused, scratching day-old chin stubble. "*And*, if I'm not mistaken, Peppa was already in the oven."

Things were hopeless when they talked about her as if she were a blind and deaf mound of bone and flesh propped up on a chair.

"*And* if you remember, it about killed me," Patrice countered. "But now that she's made the move, we have to give her time."

"For what? Everything she needs is in this house. Food. Clothes. A *dishwasher*." He folded his arms across his chest, clearly proud of what he considered just one of their "luxury" appliances. But the refrigerator groaned. Igniters on all four gas burners had been clicking, in need of a match, for at least a decade. And the sink faucet dribbled continuously like a newborn.

"You forgot the toilet," Patrice deadpanned.

"Exactly. A toilet."

"I believe the girl wants more."

"More of what?" Declan asked.

"From life."

"What does that even *mean*?"

"If you have to ask, there's no point answering."

"Don't get cute, Patrice. She's just traveled a total of three hours in one day. And to do what? Work unholy hours. *That* is no life."

Additionally, there are other occasions when defending oneself is imperative.

"Wait a minute," Peppa broke in. "That's exactly what *you* do!"

"I run a business. You're in the steno pool."

"There's no steno pool anymore, Daddy! And . . . well . . . my boss thinks I'm good."

"He told you that? On your first day? What's he, crazy?"

"Sweet Jesus, Declan. Leave her be."

"Do you mind, Patrice? I'm conversing with my daughter."

"My boss sent me an email—" Peppa said.

His hands popped up as if stopping traffic. "Patrice, how's about you and me move to the Florida Keys. Spend down our retirement money. Because Peppa's received an *eeee*mail from Gordon Gekko himself."

Patrice stood abruptly. The chair legs caught on a flap of linoleum Declan had been promising to glue for weeks, causing the chair to tip over. She walked to the overflowing laundry basket in the corner of the kitchen and grabbed a pair of his soiled briefs. She wadded them into a ball and aimed. He ducked, and they landed on top of the microwave, an appliance he'd forgotten to include on Peppa's *Life of Ryan* list.

"Must you torture the child so?" Patrice said while righting the chair. She resumed the Sudoku for a few seconds before crumpling it in her fist. "Numbers. I can't concentrate. Which reminds me—that kitchen job in Woodside? The client called this afternoon. Insists we've miscalculated something."

"Impossible. Peppa did that budget. I'd stake my life on it."

"Not the budget. Dimensions. He says something's off by three inches."

"Did he say what?"

"No. You'll have to stop by tomorrow."

"We closed that job out over a month ago. Pull the plans and I'll take a look."

Patrice emitted a rare chuckle. "I reorganized the office last week. Now I'm not sure where anything is. I don't know why I bother."

Offering assistance, even unsolicited, can be an act of mercy.

"It's Mr. Schmitt, right?" Peppa asked.

"The very one," Patrice said.

"He's referring to the change he wanted in the planning stage over a year ago. He insisted on raising the counter height by three inches. But he's really short, and now that the stone's been installed, he probably realizes he made a mistake. Anyway, the change is noted on page three of the plans. I redlined and dated it. Then if you go to the spec sheet, I think at the bottom of page seven, the mill worker confirmed: *Client requests raising counter height contrary to industry standards.*"

"That's right! And I warned him not to do it," Declan said. "Arrogant little sod."

"I'll pull it before I go to bed and leave it by the front door, Daddy. And Mom, you stashed all the plans from the last three months in the bin behind the tall filing cabinet."

"Our girl," Declan said, flicking his thumb her way. "What're we gonna do without her?"

After she'd showered and slipped between her sheets, Peppa reached over and switched off the bare bulb hanging from the ceiling. Light from the moon cast a cold grey onto the walls of her bedroom. For her fifth birthday, they'd painted them a shade of pink she couldn't live without. The color had long since faded to a dull peach she could barely tolerate. She struggled to get comfortable. The mattress her dad purchased at a closeout sale had begun to sag the very first week of use. She flopped onto her back and sidled to one side, trying to avoid the divot. Finally her body went slack, but her mind wouldn't quit. Among many things, she worried about what to wear the next day. Certainly not a reprise of the pencil skirt. A few outfits, all along the lines of muumuus, baggy trousers, and loose-fitting blouses, smothered a wicker chair her mom had recently rescued from the next-door neighbors' trash heap. Peppa had already decided to leave extra early the next morning, so she'd just grab the one that happened to be on top of the pile. It didn't much matter what she wore, so long as there was no tight waistband to remind her of the pounds she was forever trying to lose.

Now a damp wind ripped through the window casing. Her dad had never bothered to insulate them, and she could smell, almost taste, ocean salt as if sitting on a bench a few feet from the surf. In fact, the entire house, which had begun life as a summer bungalow more than fifty years ago, was pretty much one storm away from major destruction. But the floors were the worst. Conversations, difficult or benign, floated up through wide gaps in the floorboards. She could hear them talking in the kitchen below.

"You talked to the doctor?" he asked.

"The nurse."

"And?"

"She said to increase the dosage."

"But the side effects."

"It's a trade-off I'll have to live with."

"Patrice—"

"We've been here before. The voices will leave. I'll settle down."

"But when you don't answer the phone for hours on end, what would you have me think?"

"Think nothing. I'm getting the work done."

"This is bleedin' well not about work, and you know it."

"Work helps. It focuses me. And will you *please* stop using my troubles as a tool against Peppa."

"She has a responsibility to us. To you."

"Let her play it out. Your daughter is entitled to have a dream or two. We had them once ourselves."

Just how many of their dreams had been dashed, Peppa didn't exactly know. But she did understand that her parents were a miracle, because they'd come from crushing poverty. Both had been pulled from grade school to work on farms. At fifteen, they'd faked their ages to marry in secret. Then with just a phone number of a distant relation, they'd scrounged enough money, landed in New York City, and taken a bus to a place called Sandy Point. They were earnest people who never took for granted the humble life they'd carved for themselves. Her mom, a faded beauty with a bird-thin waist and perfectly arched eyebrows, was a gorgeous storyteller, and throughout her early childhood, Peppa heard a million tales of their life before she was born. But when the multiple voices took hold in her mom's head, everything they'd ever dreamt of flew out of their orbit.

"This is no time for her *dreams*," Declan said. "I'm worried about you."

"I'm fine."

"You're not."

"I will be once the drugs kick in. Give it another week."

"She needs to know what's been happening—"

"*No*, Declan. You're not to tell her about my latest."

"But I need her. I'm behind. Scrabbling like a crab in heat. For God's sake, Patrice, she does the bloody payroll."

"I tell you, she's not to be bothered."

Peppa heard a loud noise and figured her mom must have slammed something on the table to press the point. Silence held, until she heard one of them crying. She couldn't tell which.

"Promise me, Declan."

He blew his nose. "Yes. Fine. But what in God's name happened today?"

"They told me to go to the beach."

"That's all?"

"Sit on that bench."

"I don't like the sound of *that*."

"Walk naked into the water."

"Sweet lord, Patrice."

"But I didn't do it, did I. Took a pill. Slept the rest of the day."

"But don't you see? With Peppa away, I have no way of keeping track of you. It's like being in purgatory."

"I haven't obeyed the voices for quite a while."

"That's only because she's *been here*."

"I'm in control."

"Patrice. Seriously?"

"Leave me be, Declan."

Peppa hugged her knees to her chest, thinking about what she understood only too well—the hardships her parents would face, and all because she was leaving. Her mom's mental illness, and the voices she heard, inflicted torment—demanding that she perform strange, and at times dangerous, acts. They'd been kept at bay with difficult-to-tolerate medication, but this rendered her mom housebound and feeling without purpose. And then, almost like responding to an internal calendar with a particular day marked with a star, she'd declare herself perfectly fine and stop the drugs. But Patrice Ryan would never, ever, be fine.

What a strange thing, to know all about her mom's voices, but never let on about her own. Peppa's voice first manifested when she was about six, but spoke infrequently. Then a few years later, and as a precocious young reader, Peppa became fixated on Clarissa, the heroine of the novel *Mrs. Dalloway*. She immediately decided that the voice in her head, with its unhurried and upper-crust British accent, could only belong to Virginia Woolf.

Now she heard her parents pad up the stairs. Their bedroom door clicked shut. They rustled around in the adjacent room. Then the bedsprings croaked and finally, the house went silent. Peppa stared out the window, to the full moon, to the clouds that passed in front of it, to the blue-black sky that surrounded it all.

And she thought, *Dear Virginia, we are not like my mom.*

SISTER KIT

THE MOMENT IVAN LEARNED THAT PEPPA HAD NEVER EATEN A LOBSTER, HE'D begun prepping her for what he guaranteed would be a life-changing experience. Now they stood just inside the entrance to The Shell restaurant, where an enormous water tank housed many dozens. Peppa assessed the situation. Their gigantic claws had been handcuffed with red rubber bands, so even if they had room, they couldn't move more than an inch in either direction. And who in their right mind would imagine that a display like this could entice anyone to eat one of these poor creatures.

Ivan seemed to sense her confusion. "They're in the crustacean family," he explained. "Like shrimp."

Not knowing how to respond, she could only shake her head in disbelief.

"I can understand never having had lobster, but surely you've eaten shrimp," he continued blithely.

"I admit I haven't."

"Filet of sole? It's quite mild."

"Not that I remember."

"Oh, c'mon. What about swordfish. That's about as generic as meatloaf."

"Ivan, my parents didn't grow up eating fish. I think the first time they saw a body of water was from a plane when they crossed the Atlantic to move here. My mom cooks meat only."

"But you live by the ocean. Not even fish and chips at your local diner? Not that that counts as anything resembling a fish."

"My dad doesn't believe in wasting money on restaurants when my mom can just as easily prepare food at home."

"Sounds a bit rigid."

"We never splurge on specialties."

"Food isn't a *specialty*. It's basic. Like clothing. A house."

How could she reasonably explain, much less justify, the way they lived? "They're just careful about money," she said softly, hoping to put the subject to rest.

"I suppose you *could* call lobster a specialty food—I'll give you that. But today we're going to splurge. You've sailed through your first four weeks brilliantly, and I guarantee this will be a celebratory meal you'll never forget."

She stared again at the lobsters, in misery. A few were squished together in a way that made them look like they were having a group prayer session. Or begging for their life. But if Peppa understood Ivan correctly, very soon one of these goners would be on her plate. Dead.

The hostess greeted Ivan by name and ushered them through the mobbed restaurant. She pulled the table out, and Ivan gestured for Peppa to sit. "Take the banquette so you can enjoy the room."

While Ivan excused himself to visit the restroom, Peppa examined a huge painted mural on the opposite wall, mostly shades of blues and greens, obviously intended as the color of the ocean. The sea creature pushing up through a wave didn't resemble an anatomically correct fish, more like a bloated cartoon. Lighting fixtures were suspended from thick ship ropes, drawing her eye up so as to appreciate the enormously high ceilings. She imagined all of this was meant to create the illusion of lying face-up on a raft in a pool, or on the deck of a boat in the middle of the ocean, neither of which she'd ever experienced. And she could almost buy into it, except that at ground level the tables were set much too close, with less than a foot between. No wonder the place was a cacophony of jumbled conversations.

The table to their left was empty, so she couldn't help but overhear a breakup in progress on her right. The woman had just placed her head in her hands, a gesture signaling a certain misery Peppa often succumbed to herself, though having nothing to do with romance. The man reached over and tried to stroke the woman's hair, but she jerked back. Then he reassured her that he *still liked her*. From this phrase, Peppa could reasonably deduce that he'd professed his love at some point in the past. Maybe as recently as the night before, because he looked like the squirrely type who could be that cruel. Then Peppa thought, if somebody loved you, wouldn't they *always* love you? That's what Whitney Houston sang in "Where Do Broken Hearts Go." So, the squirrel's declaration of *still liking her* didn't mirror a universal truth enshrined in a hit song. The public certainly wouldn't stand for the squirrel's flip-flopping, so why should this woman? Now she was bawling her head off while the squirrel began to whisper-plead that they should stay friends. Take walks. Go on day trips. She could *cook him dinner*. All the things they'd done before the *love* thing happened. Suddenly the woman threw a few bills on the table and walked out. The squirrel pocketed the money and signaled for another drink. If this was the way relationships ended—in a crowded restaurant, sitting opposite a rodent, shoving food around your plate while weeping openly—Peppa would stick to hearing about it solely via Whitney's prodigious vocal chops. Not that the possibility would ever present itself.

The waiter appeared just as Ivan returned, and he immediately ordered for them both. A martini for himself, a Diet Coke for her. Soup to begin. Then, two female lobsters weighing one and a half pounds each. These details perplexed Peppa, and it must have shown on her face.

"The meat is most tender in females under two pounds," he explained.

"Ivan, I have to warn you . . . I don't think I'm going to like it."

"Look. I know many who love it. And even a few who can't go a month without it. But I don't know a soul who doesn't at least *like* lobster. I wish I could describe the flavor to you, but there's no other food remotely similar. But it does have the texture of a perfectly roasted chicken, so surely you can imagine that. Anyway, The Shell is the best in the city. In less diligent hands, it's easy to mess up the scalding process."

"*Scalding?*"

"It's actually pretty simple. You plunge the lobster into boiling water while it's still alive. Then you watch the pot like mad in order to pull it out the moment it turns bright red."

Peppa frowned. "Sounds awful. And cruel."

He shrugged as if the procedure were as harmless as shredding a head of lettuce. "There's no pain involved."

"How can you know that?"

"All the experts say they can't feel anything. When they hit the water there's a hissing sound. But that's just air being forced out of the holes in their bodies."

"Excuse me, but that could be their version of a scream. Due to *pain*," Peppa said.

"They don't have vocal cords. And in about three seconds they're goners. Anyway, think about the meat your mom cooks. Slaughterhouses? Now *there's* some serious pain."

"Okay, you've got a point there. But what about that tank by the entrance. It's like a prison. How long do they have to live that way—all crammed together? For days?"

"The entire tank gets eaten every day. The restaurant displays them like that as an assurance that they're as fresh as possible. They're flown in each morning from coastal Maine."

"Delivered in a plane? That's nuts."

"It's a tradition for most upscale seafood restaurants. And not just New York. The West Coast too."

"But that can't possibly be cost effective."

"Did you notice the price tag?" he asked.

"You ordered before I even got a chance to open the menu."

He laughed. "I guess I did run the show. But I'm pretty sure The Shell covers all expenses and makes a tidy profit."

He seemed to have an answer for everything, which didn't surprise her, because so far there wasn't a subject that had come up, no matter how obscure, that Ivan wasn't conversant on. Still, Peppa was about to challenge him again on the cost ratio aspect when their first course of tomato soup arrived, and she was famished. So she dropped the topic and took a sip.

"Hey. This is *cold*," she said. "And really spicy."

"It's gazpacho."

"Oh yeah. Right," she said, nodding slowly.

"You've never had gazpacho soup before."

"Just Campbell's," she admitted with a sigh. "On spaghetti. My mom uses it as the sauce."

"What a novel idea," he deadpanned.

Was he making a snarky joke at her expense? But it *was* pretty ridiculous, because who else but her mom would open a can of soup when she could just as easily pour Ragu from a jar?

Ivan raised his glass. "Here's to tomato soup, whether gazpacho or Campbell's. And here's to lobster. But most of all, here's to you, Peppa."

She air-clinked back, a gesture she'd seen in lots of movies but never had reason to do in her own life. "Ivan, this restaurant. The food. It's all so fancy. I'm not used to it," she murmured.

"You must have gone to *some* nice places. What about for celebrations? Like when you graduated as high school valedictorian."

"I saw something interesting in *The Daily Sangram*. That's the Bangladeshi newspaper I told you I've been keeping track of—the English version. There was an article about the competing toilet company. They've filed for bankruptcy, so it looks like we'll be clear of any muddle. Good news!"

Ivan said nothing.

"Right?"

"That was quite a non sequitur," he said. "You didn't celebrate your graduation?"

She looked down into her bowl. It was the most delicious soup she'd ever tasted. **Speaking embarrassing truths aloud often lessens their power.**

"They didn't attend. Too busy."

"I'm sorry I brought it up, Peppa."

"It's okay. But like I said, we don't go to restaurants."

The waiter showed up, a welcomed interruption, and began to clear the table for the next course. Wet towels shaped like fish fins were laid next to each place setting. Then he took two thin plastic bibs from his pocket and tied them around their necks. Protective gear? Peppa couldn't imagine what she was in for.

"I've been thinking about your parents' farming background," Ivan said. "I grew up on a farm too."

"*What?*" she blurted out. This seemed impossible.

"It's true," he said, laughing at her outburst. "In Belarus. That's where I'm from."

"No way. You were born there? They have farms there?"

"I was. And they do."

"You don't have an accent. In fact, you sound like the six o'clock news."

"Good to hear," he said. "That's something I've tried very hard to cultivate."

"But why?"

"Shame."

"I don't get it. What would you have to be ashamed of?"

He paused for several seconds. "I had a peculiar upbringing. It's not something

I talk about very often."

"Tell me," Peppa urged. "That is, if you want to."

"I do want to. For the last month, I've seen how well you've integrated yourself into a totally new environment. It's like you have the ability to shape-shift on the spot to accommodate what I need. You'd be surprised how egocentric people can be without even realizing it. Everyone wants to stand out, be a star. It's one of the main reasons I've gone through so many assistants. But that's not what I need, and you seem to understand this. The irony is, you actually *are* a star, Peppa. But most importantly, I trust you."

"I don't know what to say."

"Nothing to say. But here goes. The farm. We weren't *regular* farmers. Nothing was sold as you might assume. It was strictly subsistence. We chopped what we grew and roasted what we slaughtered. When material goods were needed, my parents bartered, or they scrounged from the various agencies. Which is another way of saying that I was brought up deeply poor. But I didn't know what I didn't have. And I certainly didn't understand what I needed. We kids—there were ten of us—worked the farm from the time we could walk. Our land was very much off the grid, with neighbors many miles away. And because education was never a priority, most of us fell through the cracks in terms of school. The fact is, I couldn't read or write until about, oh, eight or nine. I can't recall which."

"No school. How could that be?"

"You'd be surprised, especially in Eastern European countries. But then something happened. A group of Orthodox Catholic nuns started coming around. Probably found out about us because my mother routinely raided their donation coffers. They were doing good works, checking in on families who lived in the rural areas. Of course, the real reason was to convert us. They always brought sweets as enticements for us kids to hang around and learn about all the good stuff that would happen if we believed in God. But like many in Belarus whose parents took on the state atheism of the Soviet era, I didn't grow up with any sort of religion. And what the nuns told us about Jesus was hard to take seriously. I remember thinking the Bible was a much-too-complicated story with a really sad ending. Anyway, once the nuns realized our conversion was hopeless, they dumped us. But there was one nun who'd taken an interest in me."

Ivan's story was interrupted by the arrival of the lobsters, and Peppa was freshly horrified by how bizarre they looked, their rigid bodies splayed across stark white plates. Beady eyes beneath long feelers. Claws all out of proportion and spikes protruding from every flap. And where was this so-called tender meat? No doubt somewhere inside, but she couldn't imagine hacking into this poor thing, even dead.

"Watch me. I'll demonstrate," Ivan suggested. He cracked the skeleton open with a small pair of pliers and then excavated some flesh with a two-tined fork. Peppa thought this seemed an awful lot of bother for a single bite. Then he dipped the shred in melted butter. But instead of feeding himself, he reached across the table and offered her the first bite.

Peppa scowled and shook her head. "Uh-uh."

"Open up."

"Do I have to?"

"Do you want to keep your job?" he asked mischievously.

When the meat landed on her tongue, her first impression was that it wasn't nearly as repugnant as she'd feared. Then as she chewed, she had to agree—a nicely roasted chicken. But it was when she swallowed that the totality of the flavor hit pay dirt. "Wow," she said with no small amount of astonishment.

"See what I mean?"

"I *do*."

"C'mon. Let's dig into these water puppies."

For the next twenty minutes or so, Peppa mimicked Ivan's manipulations—cracking, pulling, digging, scraping, sucking. Mopping grease off her face with the damp cloth. At one point she asked the waiter for a fresh bib because her technique was somewhat unrefined—downright chaotic, in fact. Bits of lobster flew in every direction, and Ivan laughed at her the entire time. Peppa didn't mind at all because it *was* pretty funny. Soon enough, the lunch rush receded, the place emptied out, and save for a few drinkers lingering at the bar, they were alone. The waiter cleared their plates and presented dessert menus.

"We won't need those," Ivan said, handing them back. "Bring us one order of *panna cotta* and one Meyer lemon pudding. Double espresso for me. Peppa? How do you like your caffeine?"

"Oh, regular will do."

"There's no such thing as *regular* coffee. At least not in my world. Bring her a cappuccino with two squirts of dark chocolate," he instructed the waiter. "And don't use milk. Steam some half-and-half."

"Wait," Peppa said, catching the waiter by the arm. "Ivan, I'm trying to be careful."

"Careful?"

"Well, the soup and lobster were quite filling. Now dessert. And that coffee sounds at least five hundred calories. I need to watch my figure."

"Oh, for God's sake. One fancy meal isn't going to blow this calorie-bank craze you've bought into. It's preposterous."

She slipped her hand under the table and pinched at her stomach through the blousy muumuu she'd worn—checking to see if she'd suddenly gained a pound after just one filling meal. "And shouldn't we get back to the office? We've been here over two hours."

"Hey, I'm the boss. I get to say when we work and when we goof off. As I ordered, please," he said to the waiter, waving him away. "Anyway, I haven't finished the farm story."

"Okay, okay. Keep going."

"Good. So, a bit about this nun. She was young—I'd guess mid-twenties. Not mean like those hags. If our attention veered for one second, they'd swat us. *My* nun was genuinely sweet. And pretty. She continued to visit, but it was specifically me she came to see. And whenever she arrived, my mother would call me in from the field with a cowbell."

"Were your siblings jealous?"

"I wasn't aware. But they must have been. None of them had been given such latitude with regard to work. Looking back, I think my mother viewed the nun's interest in me as a reflection on herself—special by association. Anyway, this nun was quite the renegade because she didn't preach to me about Jesus and Mary and Joseph, or Adam and Eve and the apple and original sin. None of that stuff. In fact, I was the one doing most of the talking, which was surprising because I'd always been the introvert of the family. But with her, I turned into quite a blabbermouth. She asked a lot of questions. And she listened. Nobody had ever paid that much attention to me."

"I'm sure your intelligence was obvious, so it makes sense that she'd want to draw you out. How old were you?"

"When I started hanging out with her? Eleven. I remember the age specifically because shortly after we began our visits, I broke both big toes."

"Good lord. How?"

"Well, we often didn't have enough shoes to go around, so we'd rotate depending on the chore. The day of the accident, everyone doing field work wore the shoes. I happened to be working the tractor, so I went barefooted."

"You were *eleven* and they let you operate a tractor?"

"I know. Very risky for a kid. But don't get the wrong idea. My parents taught me the logistics until they were satisfied I could work it with skill. Truly, Peppa, they weren't bad people."

Peppa couldn't hide her disapproval. "You put a nice spin on it, but it sounds like forced labor."

"I can see why you'd think that, but it never *felt* like that. Maybe because I had nothing to compare it to. Anyway, the accident itself was completely my fault. That day, I decided to jump off the tractor. A pretty fair height, plus I was small for my age. I took a flying leap, lost my equilibrium mid-flight, and landed directly on the ends of my toes—both feet."

"Ouch!"

"Yeah, they pretty much shattered on the spot. I couldn't move them or step on the balls of my feet for weeks. Needless to say, it was painful. And I was immensely bored. That is until the nun showed up, and quite a lot."

"I already love the nun," Peppa said.

"A real sweetie, she was. She brought novels and we'd read to each other, which was how I came to learn English. Whenever we finished a book, she'd always ask me to think of a different ending and write it down. She'd correct grammar and make suggestions. We had fun. I smiled more. Laughed a lot. There was a whole cluster of complex emotions operating that I'd not felt or expressed before. But it was discovering other worlds through reading that really set me free."

"Did you understand any of this at the time? Or only now, in retrospect."

"I knew it then. In the moment. My mind was erupting. I could barely contain myself. But I kept it from the rest of my family. So, I guess there was some trepidation operating too. Then, when my toes finally mended, the nun arrived with a present—a spectacular pair of boots. Kind of perfect, right? And they were extremely well made. Good leather, thick soles. The toes had been reinforced with metal—I remember finding that funny. They were at least a size too big, but she showed me how to stuff rags into the toe area so I could wear them while I grew into them. I was quite in love with my boots."

The waiter interrupted again to deliver the sweets and caffeine. Ivan took several quick sips of espresso and then pointed to the cappuccino, which she'd not touched.

"Taste that thing. You'll flip."

"But there's a pretty curlicue on top. A *lobster*. Kind of a shame to destroy it."

"Peppa. Just drink the bloody coffee!"

She took a gulp. While the liquid slid down her throat like syrup, she noticed how the chocolate tempered the espresso.

"You like?" he asked.

"I think I love."

Ivan rolled his eyes. "Oh, ye of little faith."

She alternated the desserts—sweet, then tart, then back to sweet. Guilt and pleasure vacillated. When their plates had been scraped clean, Ivan blotted the corners of his lips. He twisted his ring so that the red stone sat just so, and then laid his palm on the table. He stared at it, as if remembering, or acknowledging, what it meant to him. Now Peppa suspected that the boots had walked him directly toward that ring.

"Come on, Ivan," she prompted. "Boots."

"Yes. The boots are important. But first I need to tell you about the woods that happened to abut our land. We weren't allowed to go into this forest. Sounds like a Grimm cliché, but one time an older brother got lost for an entire day. I was too young to remember anything about it, but knowing how curious kids are, my parents warned us regularly. But here I was. My toes felt fine. I could walk again. And after being lame for so long, that forest looked pretty damned enticing."

"Oh God, *nooo!*"

"Yes. I was a very bad boy. I snuck into the forest at every opportunity. The ground was covered with brittle twigs and fallen branches. Roots that poked up through the soil. So, it would have been impossible to navigate, certainly barefooted, but also with the worn-out shoes we owned. Most had holes in the soles. But thanks to the nun, I had my boots. And God, how I loved the place. It was so different from our sunbaked farm—everything lined up in monotonous row after row after row. The forest was cool and dark. I could barely see sky through the thick pine trees. It was disorganized in a way that felt somewhat scary, but also thrilling. And something else. With a family our size, it was next to impossible to be alone. We ate meals together. The kids slept in just two rooms, and no one had a bed to themselves. One bathroom for the lot of us. And we typically worked in teams. But in the forest, I could hear myself breathe, listen to my thoughts. And for the first time in my life, I began to understand myself as individuated—not a family cog."

"Did the nun know what you were doing?"

"Not at first. But eventually she did."

Suddenly Peppa's palms began to sweat, and her mouth went bone-dry. "Wait, Ivan."

"What?"

"Please don't make me cry."

"Why on earth would you cry?"

"I'm afraid. I can't help it. Nothing ever works out," she said quietly.

"Ach, Peppa. What am I to do with you? We just had a fantastic lunch of lobster, and you loved it. That worked out. We're celebrating the fact that you've accomplished amazing work for me—superior to anything I could have imagined. *That* worked out. There are no boogie men. Not in this restaurant, or my office. Or even this story. Because that worked out too. Hey, *I'm here.*"

I've come to accept that believing the obvious is just one indication of sanity.

Right, Virginia. Peppa took a few deep breaths and shook her hands out.

"Onward?" Ivan asked.

"Yeah, I'm good."

"So. You likely understand by now that the forest was where I wanted to spend all my time. No?"

"Makes sense. I would too."

"Well, I actually wanted to *live* there. But it was a forest. So naturally I needed to work this little problem out."

"I cannot even imagine."

"You're right about that," he said with a grin. "I pilfered a rake and a saw from our work shed and cleared a good-sized area. Then I covered the ground with moss, like carpeting. For a few days I lay on the moss, thinking, trying to figure out how to build a house out of tree limbs. I didn't have the stature or the muscles to maneuver long and heavy branches. So, I knew I couldn't work large scale. I had to use branches from the ground that I could easily cut to size. Nailing them together would have been nice, but I couldn't find nearly enough nails in the shed. That's when I came up with my method. Stacking and interlocking. The basic premise was that each branch would be dependent on the one before and then support the one to come. That's a huge simplification, of course. And it wasn't simple or even easy. I ran into all manner of obstacles. Most branches were bent, so I tried shaving down the angles with the saw. That was delicate work. And it didn't work much of the time because the branch then became weakened at the area of the angle. So I had to find straighter branches, and this meant scouring a wider circumference. Then there were the animals who messed up the progress when I wasn't there—mostly beavers who stole a good portion of my nicely stacked wood for their nearby dam. These were setbacks. But nothing deterred me, because I could visualize the whole thing in my head. Finished and in 3-D."

She stared at him, gobsmacked, mouth ajar. This was completely nuts. And utterly fantastic. Ivan was her mental doppelgänger; their brains operated in exactly the same way—literally seeing dimensionality from an imagined perspective.

Dear Virginia, Peppa thought, *are you getting all this?*

Ivan went on. "I got the so-called house completed in a few weeks. I say *so-called* because it had only three sides and a roof that stood less than a foot above my head. Then I made a small chair in a scale correct for my eleven-year-old body. At that point I decided to stop, and spent the next week just sitting in *my* chair under *my* roof. Alone. And thrilled about it."

"I can almost feel it, Ivan. Privacy is difficult, even in a family of three like mine."

"Exactly. And it was my first experience making decisions. Doing the stuff I wanted to do and in the way I wanted to do it. With farming, it's all by rote, repetitive. Anyway, by this time I had my method down pat, so I assembled a table in short order. Then I was ready for the nun."

"Hold on. Before you continue, I want to know how it was that your parents allowed you to be absent from the farm so much of the time."

"They never knew. I'd hit the field each morning and then after a while wander off on some pretext of getting a tool or going to the bathroom. I'd come back a few hours later. No one paid any attention. But just in case, I always entered and exited the forest from different locations."

"Sneak extraordinaire," she observed.

"Indeed."

"Okay, your nun. She must have been blown away."

"I remember that day very well. And yeah, she *oohed* and *aahed* a lot. Then the following day, she returned with a camera to take pictures. What happened next is the reason I'm sitting here, in this restaurant, celebrating *you*."

"And wearing that ring."

He looked at his hand. "Hmmm. You're right."

"So tell me!"

"Lego."

Again, Peppa couldn't believe what she was hearing. "You mean . . . *Lego?*"

"Yes. Lego. The nun sent the photos to the main headquarters in Denmark. I later found out she'd addressed the envelope with just two words: *Lego* and *Denmark*. Like Santa Claus and North Pole. Well, the nun's pictures not only got to the company, but to the president of Lego himself. After some back and forth, he came down to inspect my work. It seemed my house and furniture were not just good; they were *impeccably* built. Perfectly symmetrical. Aesthetically pleasing. In short, spectacular. I had no idea what all these words being thrown about meant. Or why this was even such a big deal. But the nun and Mr. Kristiansen began conspiring to get me off the farm. It was relatively easy to convince my parents because Mr. K. found benefactors who committed to stake me however far I wanted to go—even through grad school."

"This is like winning the Lotto."

"It really was. And the farm did perfectly fine without my set of hands, but my transition in Denmark was up and down. I was pretty scared, what with being thrust into a totally unfamiliar environment. Everything was new. The land itself was strange, and the language sounded like people had rocks in their mouths. Good thing many Danes spoke English. It was a mighty learning curve. I went in and out of homesickness. But I was with good people who gave me not only financial support, but were also kind and nurturing. I adapted, slipped a few times, and got a first-rate education along the way. All because of the nun and her boots."

"That is an incredible story. But what happened to her?"

"She quit the nunnery and married a former priest. They had kids. Grandkids. And she stayed fairly religious but was relieved to live a secular life. She died about ten years ago. We kept up the entire time. Sister Katherine was her name. Kit for short, and Irish. For some reason, the archdiocese sent her to Belarus. And am I ever glad they did."

It was by this time late afternoon, and the waiters had begun transitioning the tables for the dinner rush. There was no point going back to the office, so Ivan hailed a cab. Peppa shoved herself into a packed subway, and then was lucky to snag the last seat on the bus.

Luck is a thing deeper than happenstance; I suspect it is, many times, predicated on one's readiness to receive it.

Peppa thought, *Maybe that's true, Virginia.*

But luck was also a concept her parents always scoffed at. Her dad insisted that only idiots believed that lucky stars caused workers to arrive on time and clients to behave like sane people. And according to her mom, an aligned universe was an absurd notion, because no one and nothing were *ever* at the right place at the right time. Then she remembered how Ivan had almost scolded her when she assumed his story was headed toward tragedy and would cause her to cry. And he was right to set her straight because if she had been paying closer attention, she'd have noticed that there'd been no foreboding in his eyes, no indication of an oncoming train wreck in his voice. In fact, he seemed to be having the time of his life telling her about the farm, the nun, the boots, and his bravery. And yes, his good luck.

Peppa stepped off the bus and as she approached her house, she could hear it and feel it—her parents' pessimistic drumbeat that dominated the rhythm of her life. They'd always admonished her not to waste time striving for better, but just to aim for good enough. To hope for nothing, expect the worst, and settle for whatever came. These were their rules for living a resigned and very small life, and she'd never had much of a reason to question it until now. Because during the lunch with Ivan, she'd learned a few things, both unexpected and wonderful. Lobster was indeed worthy of delivery by JetBlue. And coffee with chocolate would forevermore be her morning drink of choice. Yes, there was all of this, but also something even better. Her brain and Ivan's brain were cut from the same, very weird, cloth. It was why he'd hired her. It was why she hadn't run out of the office that first day. It was why their work *was* going to change the world. And maybe, all of it was meant to be.

And Peppa thought, *Dear Virginia, do you believe in fate too?*

NO ONE IN THE WORLD

"MOM . . . I'M LEAVING," PEPPA CALLED TOWARD THE OFFICE. IT WAS JUST PAST dawn, and her mom had been at her desk poring over the big Manhattan job for at least an hour. As it turned out, the project involved decorative trades her parents had never worked with before. Venetian plasterers, French gilders, architectural metal fabricators from New Mexico. Even a Japanese tatami mat guy who happened to live in Dusseldorf. Coordinating time zones for conference calls proved confusing enough. But even more challenging had been negotiating how to weave unfamiliar production lead times into what was the routine construction flow her parents had followed for years. And after completing a third month at her job, where she continued to transcribe the nutty words of one wealthy client after another, it came as no surprise to Peppa that her parents were also being driven crazy by *their* rich client. It seemed he changed his mind about every third day. Endless phone calls ensued. Change orders flew back and forth. Then, because the budget had to get rejiggered, work stopped cold while the client haggled about the price and then complained about the delays he himself was causing. Yet, despite good money coming in from the windfall project, her parents weren't thriving in the way Peppa had hoped they would. Her dad was more irascible than usual, and her mom had devolved into neglecting to shower, wearing just a bathrobe all day long.

"Answer, for God's sake," Peppa muttered to herself, then yelled, "Mother! I'm saying goodbye to you!"

Patrice emerged from the office and motioned listlessly to the kitchen table. Her eyes looked vacant, almost haunted. "Sit. We need to talk."

"The guy's waiting out there. Can't it hold till tonight?"

"No."

"Mom, the company's paying for the car service."

"They can afford it."

"I have a really tight morning," Peppa whined, standing her ground. "A new client. And he's famous."

"Goody for him. He'll live," Patrice said, jamming clumps of stringy hair behind her ears.

Peppa went to the front door and waved to the driver. "I'll be right out!"

"No, get rid of him," her mom called from the kitchen.

"I'll see if he'll wait, because I'm leaving in five minutes. Max."

It was only recently that she'd summoned her courage and dangled the idea of a car service to Ivan. He immediately agreed, and just like that her dreary commute had vanished. By luck, this driver lived close by and as the fare was meaty, he agreed to arrive preemptively at the same time each morning.

"What's up, Peppa?" the driver asked.

"I'm really sorry. I've got to talk to my mom for a few minutes."

"I can wait," he offered with a yawn.

The gutted look that had been on her mom's face indicated that *a few minutes* was, most likely, a fantasy. "No. I'll get a cab on Beach Road. See you tomorrow." She handed him a ten to soften the blow of lost revenue, then watched him roll down the street only to pick up a fare at the end of the block.

When she returned to the kitchen, tea was steeping in a pot. Her mom sat at the table, rocking slightly to a silent beat. Peppa slipped into the opposite chair and stretched her hands across the table. Her mom grabbed on, weak when she meant strong.

"You're worse?" Peppa asked tentatively.

"Not as bad as you think. I went up on the blue pill, so the tremors are better." She lifted her hands to demonstrate. Only the right index finger flickered.

"So, what's this about? The big job?"

"No. But now that you mention it, that client. What a misery. Here he is rich as Croesus, but I guarantee that man wouldn't lose a wink bilking his own mother out of pin money. The pettiness is off the charts. Wealthy people. Who raised them?"

Peppa laughed. "I can relate. We've got a ton at LBS."

"Pour the tea. And get rid of that awful device," she said, pointing to Peppa's phone. "The sun's barely up and it's blinking like it needs new friends."

Her mom's irritation was palpable, and Peppa suspected that another lecture having to do with the rest of her life was about to be delivered. Starting with *admit to the foolishness of the last three months and rejoin the family business.* Followed by *go on dates with a bunch of guys in the construction trades.* Then *marry one,* though it wouldn't much matter which one. Finally, after nine months and one week, she'd birth their first grandbaby and the Ryan dynasty would be assured of a successor.

Peppa messaged Ivan—*I might be late, family stuff*—and received an immediate *OK.* After dropping the phone into her purse, she poured the tea.

"It's Maloney," Patrice said, looking through the window above Peppa's head in the direction of their neighbors' house down the block.

"What about him?" Peppa didn't care for any of them. Actually, God-awful people.

Patrice nodded as if reading her mind. "Hold on there. Not him. Not exactly. It's the nephew."

Peppa squirmed in her seat. "Oh shit."

"Will you simply listen for one minute?"

"Here we go." Peppa twirled her finger around. "Yippeee!"

"He came over a few months ago. A plumber. Your father's been working him into the rotation—"

"Oh, come *on,* Mother."

"By all accounts the guy's doing really well and your father and I think you should—"

The word *should* implies some manner of aggression, and usually leads to some measure of regret.

"*No.*" Peppa gripped the edge of the table, breaking one of her nails at the quick. She clamped the fragment between her teeth, pulled, and blew it across the table. Blood poured immediately. "Now look," she said, licking red. "And they were just getting decent."

Patrice handed her a crumpled tissue from her robe pocket. Peppa wrapped the finger and applied pressure as if staunching a gunshot wound.

"Lord, daughter. Such a little actress."

"I wish I could act myself right out of the bucket of blood you're about to dump on my head. Just call me Carrie."

"Who? And ungrateful too."

"No, Mom. Grateful as all hell. But I'm finished with the matchmaking. It's a waste of time, and I feel like garbage after."

"We think he might be different."

"That is literally impossible," Peppa said, shaking her head furiously. "He's a plumber, for criminy sake."

"He's got a degree from university."

"In what, a survey of toilets throughout the Cro-Magnon period? Of which there were none? Easy A."

"His face is pleasant enough. Interesting eyes."

"This is crazy."

"Your father's been on about him for a while now, and when I met him last weekend at Maloney's daughter's bridal shower—"

"What in bloody hell was he doing at a *bridal* shower? And did I ever tell you what Melanie Maloney did to me in the bathroom in junior high?"

"The tampon episode."

"Precisely," Peppa said.

"She's . . . matured."

"She's a sub-norm with an evil streak."

Patrice shook her head, then immediately switched to nodding. "True. But Melanie's got her mother's genes. That woman couldn't assemble a ham sandwich if it oinked the recipe at her. Brendon's dad is Melanie's father's brother's son—"

"It's too early in the morning for genealogy—"

"And that strain of the family is more than acceptable."

"They're cretins. The whole sorry lot. Dumber than my left shoe."

Her mom stared at her, defeated.

Even when one is at wits' end, show empathy for those who suffer.

"Okay," Peppa said. "Tell me about this so-called genius. What're his current coordinates?"

"He's living in the room over their garage—"

"Oh, Jesus."

"Until he saves enough money to get his own place. Anyway, he wandered through and . . . actually, I think he needed to use the toilet—"

"A plumber taking a piss. Wonderful."

"Look, what I'm saying is he seemed a decent young man," Patrice said.

"How's his accent? A brogue to beat all?"

"Don't be hateful. These are our people."

Patrice clasped her hands together and mouthed some words toward the light bulb dangling from the ceiling. Well, maybe God *was* sitting on their roof listening to them fight. Peppa decided to give the big man his due and waited for her mom to make the sign of the cross before continuing.

"Mother. Do you even get what I'm saying?"

"Believe it or not, I think I do. Finally. Your father? He's another story."

"Well, he's delusional. This whole thing's gotten beyond ridiculous. Marriage is nowhere near. And *kids*?" Peppa slit her throat with an imaginary knife. "Murder the thought."

"It didn't happen for your father—all my miscarriages. He wanted a litter."

"Not. My. Fault." Peppa emphasized each word by jabbing her bloody finger on the table, causing the teacups to shudder against their saucers. "Sorry. Other plans."

"And what are these plans? You leave before sunrise. You've not had dinner with us in . . . I can't remember. No idea what you're doing, or even—" Patrice stopped mid-sentence to shiver and drew her robe up around her neck. "You might as well be living at the North Pole."

"Want me to move out?"

"Don't be provocative." Patrice gazed toward Heaven again, then returned to Earth. "Just *meet* the guy?"

"Meet him. That's it?"

"Well . . . maybe go on a date or two. If it doesn't work, and believe me I've no illusions, I'll get your father to back off. That's a promise."

This particular promise—that they'd leave her be if she dated this painter, that electrician, some carpenter—Peppa didn't believe for one second. Because historically, her mom had never been able to temper her dad's expectations, much less influence anything about the way he insisted they live—in a time warp. And it was a depressing and limiting environment that Peppa, now more than ever, meant to escape from. In fact, she was planning to move into a spare bedroom in Lorraine's apartment on the Manhattan side of the Brooklyn Bridge. Lorraine was quirky, but the opportunity popped up recently, and Peppa grabbed it. Now it occurred to her that she could actually use the plumber as leverage. If she gave him the perfunctory once-over, she could then hold her mom to her promise—that she'd satisfied the last of the first dates. Then she'd drop the moving-out bomb.

"If I'm to spend any amount of time with this guy," Peppa said, "I'll need a preliminary look."

"Of course. Just as you say."

"Tell him to come over this weekend—Sunday. While you and Dad are at Mass."

"There's Communion this Sunday. I think he's religious."

"He won't go to Hell for missing a wafer and a thimble of grape juice."

"Daughter. What has turned you so disrespectful?"

"The big bad world, I suppose."

"It's this job of yours. I pray you know what you're doing."

"You don't have to pray for me, Mom. I'm good."

"I sincerely doubt that. But come." Patrice opened the office door and beckoned to Peppa. "I need a second set of eyes on the latest whims of Prince La-di-da."

A dozen or so folders had been piled on top of the computer keyboard. Patrice reached into the pile and, like a clairvoyant, plucked out a folder labeled *Heir Apparent—Current Billing*. Peppa set to work and quickly discovered a few mistakes, redlining them for correction. Then she opened the computer and looked over some emails her mom had sent the day before, making sure the wording was appropriately neutral; at times her moods would seep into the language. But the emails seemed just fine, and Peppa found this not only a relief, but even more evidence that her plans were beginning to align. As they started back toward the kitchen, she willed herself to refrain from bugging her mom, yet again, to bring in remediation for the mold that seemed to be getting worse. Not her mold. And hopefully, very soon, not her life.

She flagged a yellow cab crawling down Beach Avenue. Assuming the driver was lost, she began advising him on the most efficient route to downtown Manhattan. But before they got out of Sandy Point, he suggested they try out the brand-new GPS device he'd installed on the dashboard. He seemed quite eager and Peppa was very tired, so she signaled two thumbs-up through the Plexiglas barrier. With navigation now off her mind, she sunk into one corner, extended her legs across the back seat, and concentrated on the morning sky through the opposite window.

It had transitioned from a grainy dawn to bulbous cumulonimbus clouds that allowed only small patches of blue to break through. These particular clouds would surely yield rain by midday. She had always appreciated how predictable clouds were, and she knew that the likelihood of precipitation from this particular formation could be trusted about 90 percent of the time. Unlike her mom, whom she trusted less than 10 percent of the time. And suddenly she realized that the odds of her mom keeping her part of the bargain were too close to zero. So, Peppa would need to destroy the plumber in such a way that there'd be no possibility of another matchmaking attempt, ever. But how?

There happens to exist the rare woman whose beauty is indisputably so profound that when gazing at her, men report a kind of scorching of the eyeballs.

Dear Virginia, Peppa thought, *do you mean someone like . . . Elizabeth Taylor?*

And at times this rare woman is so confident of the power that her beauty affords her, she feels emboldened to unleash the most scathing words imaginable towards the men whose eyeballs have, in fact, been scorched.

You mean . . . Richard Burton? Wait . . . like . . . Martha and George? In Who's Afraid of Virginia Woolf? *Dear Virginia!*

This was precisely how she'd dispatch the plumber. Like Martha, verbally ripping George to shreds. She'd be dismissive in general, condescending at tight intervals, and throw barbarous insults as the situation required. Peppa would twist the guy up so bad he wouldn't know whether to whistle "The Star-Spangled Banner" or sing "Molly Malone." She'd try to pull it off in less than an hour. And if she was terribly clever, he'd book a flight the very next day, back to Dingle or whatever dorky-sounding town he came from. Then she'd never have to see him lurking around the neighborhood, knocking on strangers' doors, asking if he could piss in their toilet. But what was his name? Brutus? Bluto? Brontë?

Brendon.

"I don't want to know his name!" she yelled toward the roof of the cab.

Sorry, Virginia, Peppa thought.

The driver hit the brakes hard. "Miss? I make good time. Yes?"

Peppa looked around. They were across from her building. "Yup. Great time."

She tipped him extra generously, because without the GPS device she wouldn't have noticed the clouds, and wouldn't have remembered how unreliable her mom was, and Virginia wouldn't have intervened with the solution, and then she wouldn't have devised the plan for getting rid of the plumber. Yes, her luck was stacking up quite nicely.

Despite the delay, she arrived with a decent chunk of time before the famous client was due to appear. She tossed her purse into a drawer and noticed a container of Starbucks chocolate cappuccino sitting on her desk. "Is this from you?" she called through the partition.

Lorraine popped up with a black comforter draped over her head, looking like the grim reaper without the scythe. "You usually show up before eight, so I figured you wouldn't have time. But look at this." She thrust a room thermometer into Peppa's face. "I'm absolutely frozen."

Peppa squinted. Fifty-eight degrees. "Yeah, that *is* chilly," she said, nodding sympathetically. For weeks Lorraine had been sending a daily email to the building management asking that the thermostat be raised to sixty-eight degrees. "Any response yet?"

"Not a peep. How can they ignore me like this?"

"It's a huge building. They must get tons of complaints every day. I mean, who knows how they get it sorted."

"I'm thinking of doubling up. Two emails a day."

"Couldn't hurt." Actually, Peppa doubted they would pay any attention to one woman in one office occupying one cubicle in the tallest building in NYC. They'd probably tagged her as a nuisance long ago and relegated her to spam.

"Did you talk to your parents?" Lorraine asked.

Peppa cocked her head. "What about?"

"Moving into my place."

"Oh, right. I meant to, but other stuff came up this morning. It wasn't the right time."

"Just as well. My landlord left a message yesterday that he's having the floors sanded and stained at the beginning of next week. *Finally*. I've only been emailing every week for six months now. "

Peppa figured . . . twenty-five emails, minimum. "Another week or so works better anyway. I need to fix a leaky pipe before I break it to my folks."

"Your parents make you do the plumbing?"

Was living with Lorraine going to include explaining every silly metaphor? "What I mean is, there's something I've got to resolve before I tell them."

"Ah. Got it."

"But I could if I had to," Peppa said.

"Could what?"

"Fix a leak."

"Good to know, because last night I sent out emails to three different plumbers for the intermittent drip underneath the kitchen sink."

"Plumbers are usually too busy for little things like that, Lorraine. Anyway, shouldn't the super fix it?"

"He's useless. A drunk."

"How bad is it?"

"His office is right next door to the laundry room. I smell alcohol every time I do a load."

"No, I mean how bad is *the drip*?"

"Oh. Well, over the weekend I clocked it at one drip every two hours. I have a bowl sitting underneath just in case."

That was twelve drips every twenty-four hours. Plus, for Lorraine to have observed this, she must have been sitting on the floor, staring into the base cabinet for an entire day. Waiting for a drip. Wow. Still, Peppa kind of admired her diligence. "Anyway, thanks for the Starbucks."

Lorraine descended behind the partition just as Ivan walked out of his office. He propped himself at the edge of Peppa's desk. "What's up?"

She scrunched her nose and shrugged.

"A morning like that?" he asked.

"Exactly like that."

"Want to tell me?"

"Maybe later. The rock star's about to arrive."

"Before you meet him, I heard from the toilet guys. About the redesign. And the financials."

"What'd they say?"

He turned away and trained his attention on the stock feed running across the monitors mounted at the ceiling.

Peppa jostled his arm. *"What?"*

"Those damned overnight markets will react to anything. Someone shoots off a firecracker at Times Square and everybody sells," he said, continuing to watch the numbers slump by the second.

"Okay. They couldn't work it out," Peppa said with resignation. "I figured as much."

Ivan finally turned to her. "You know, I find your attitude terribly annoying."

"You do? I mean, how?"

"Disappointments are part of the landscape."

"You're absolutely right. I'm sorry."

"And remember, working with nonprofits is all about the long game. You're just going to have to toughen up, Peppa. That is, if you want to survive."

Ivan had never admonished her before. She felt her heart start to pound. "Yes, yes. I will. I promise."

"By the way, do we have any party stuff lying around the kitchen?" he asked.

"You mean like candles? That sort of thing?"

"Yeah. And balloons."

"I think so. Is it someone's birthday?"

"No, you dope. *The toilets.* It's a go!"

She shoved her chair back from the desk, rolling several feet away from him. "That was *so* mean!"

"I couldn't resist. It's pretty easy to get your goose."

She shook her head slowly, letting the news sink in. "It's positively unreal."

"You nailed it, and right out of the gate, Peppa."

Hard as it was for Peppa to believe, everything *had* flowed from the data-dump she'd produced on her very first day of work—when she was dead certain she'd crash before noon. But one avenue in her research exposed what she suspected might be a flaw in the technology that the company had hung their entire system on. In the days following, as they reviewed her comments and confirmed the error, they announced that they'd need to step back and attempt a redesign. Which also meant they had to assess their financials. And while there was no guarantee that the company would be able to resurface, Peppa had, in any case, saved them hundreds of thousands of dollars by stopping production of a faulty prototype.

"I took a cursory glance at the new prospectus," Ivan said. "It looks reasonable. Of course, I'll need you to scrutinize the finer points, but we'll discuss all that at lunch. We're at the Fulton Tavern today, right?"

"Do you mind if we switch to The Shell? I'm literally dying for a lobster."

"Sure, happy to feed your newly acquired addiction."

She glanced at her watch. "Oh lord. The client's probably already in the elevator."

"Go to it. I'm very curious about his predicament."

Ivan walked back toward his office, and Peppa took note of the medium grey suit he wore over his black shirt. The cut of his jacket draped perfectly against his back, and the creases in his pant legs were like razor edges. He looked ultra-spiffy today, and she figured it was because of the rock star—a special case. Now she noticed a large food stain smack-dab on the bodice of the muumuu she'd been wearing for the last several days. Ivan never mentioned anything about her appearance, but suddenly she felt ashamed. The client was famous. The least she could have done was to wear something more presentable.

Hair is on most days a nuisance, but how one arranges it can become a signature of sorts.

Peppa thought, *Yes, Virginia. I think I get it.*

She grabbed a rubber band from her purse, bent over, shook her head vigorously, then finger-raked through tangles. Gathering up a clump at the top of her head, she secured it with the rubber band. But it didn't feel right, like she was balancing a book on her head. Then she remembered Virginia's stock style, so she started over, amassing her hair into a bun at her neck. Not having a mirror, she was certain she'd created an absurdity, and heaved a sigh. "I'm hopeless," she said to no one in particular.

"Don't worry, Peppa. You always look good," Lorraine said from the other side of the partition.

When Peppa rounded the corner to the elevator bank, there, without a doubt, was the rock star. Aviator sunglasses proved a useless disguise; in fact, his shaved head glowed as if giving off its own beacon to announce his arrival. He stood with his back against a wall, observing his fingernails from arm's length. Green sequined gloves with the fingers cut out facilitated the inspection. From his purple sneakers to his chin, he'd zippered himself into a black spandex jumpsuit. Peppa couldn't quite reconcile the spectacle standing across from her, because Garrit Flant, who in all the photographs she'd seen was as skinny as Mick Jagger, had gone enormously fat.

Peppa wiggled her fingers, catching his attention. Now he shoved his sunglasses to the crown of his head, which exposed a pair of bushy eyebrows dyed the same color as his gloves. He approached with an eager expression but as he got closer, his eyes bugged, and Peppa assumed with judgment. Maybe it was the food stains on her outfit. Or her failed attempt at a hairstyle. Whatever the case, in what felt like a mutually agreed-upon trance, they sized each other up for several seconds. Finally, Peppa extended a hand. He grabbed the tips of her fingers, then performed a surprisingly nimble curtsy, with his right leg extending in front while the left bore his weight.

"You are the impeccable Ms. Ryan, I presume? What an honor," he cooed with an accent somewhere between Cockney and the Queen.

"My pleasure, Mr. Flant. And yes, I'm Penelope. Though not nearly impeccable," she corrected.

He looked her up and down no less than three times. "I insist that you are . . . enchanting."

A lie right off the bat. Were the British all so obviously insincere, she wondered.

Regardless of one's beliefs based on nothing, it is, in most cases, best to nod and move past.

Peppa thought, *Thanks, Virginia. Professional.*

"I hope your flight was comfortable," she said.

"I fly first class," the rock star responded, "so don't you fret. And the luncheon was marvelous, beginning with popadum and chutney. Followed by saag paneer and lamb korma. All of it heaped over a double portion of basmati rice. Mango lassi for dessert. I'm *dieting*," he added in a stage whisper behind his palm, then let loose a high-pitched cackle.

Again, Peppa couldn't tell if this was a dig at her or self-deprecation, but he was so outlandish she couldn't help but smile broadly.

"My *God*," he exclaimed, moving closer to scrutinize the gap between her teeth. "One could slip no less than three confessional wafers between those front choppers.

You and I are going to get along like the Pope and his sycophants."

He'd been performing this sideshow in the middle of a busy hallway, and many who passed by did double-takes. Though all the investment firms on the floor with A-list clients enforced a strict policy of non-approach, a few fans felt emboldened to break the rules outright and ask for autographs. He seemed delighted to accommodate, so Peppa stood to the side. A fifty-something blanched visibly when Flant asked if she'd enjoyed her morning sex. He advised another that the goal of a facelift was to appear as though she'd just been roused from an afternoon nap by an illicit lover—surprise, guilt, thrill, all at once. And that her surgeon was subpar.

Interrupting a man, though by general consensus frowned upon, is always a secret joy.

"This way, Mr. Flant. Ivan is expecting us." Peppa twirled him around and pulled him down the hallway.

"Penelope!" he cried, hopping every third step to keep up. "Please! Call me GoGo!"

She stopped short and he performed a graceful sidestep, avoiding a pileup.

"GoGo?" she asked incredulously.

"What's wrong with it?" he sniffed.

"Oh dear. I guess I wasn't prepared for the . . . informality. It's a grand nickname."

"Well, well. Aren't *we* Little Miss Nose-in-the-Air Galway of 2001? And do I detect first generation?"

She beamed. "Lord, you've got a *great* ear."

"No surprise, really. I am, after all, the only guitarist alive who, even on a bad day, gave Eric Clapton a run for his polo pony. Anyway, that's what *Rolling Stone* wrote. Back when they all loved me." His head dropped, and all the bluster instantly receded.

At this point, Peppa wondered if the man suffered from a kind of harmless mania. Other than name recognition, neither she nor Ivan had known much about him until his solicitor called the previous week. He would offer no details other than his famous client was in desperate straits and needed to get out of the UK. He begged Ivan to squeeze him in. Ivan hadn't taken on a new morning client in over a year, but was sufficiently intrigued to agree to an initial meeting. In preparation, they'd stayed late a string of nights reading every article, fluff piece, and industry review on the British legend. The one filmed concert they'd managed to get their hands on captured him as the prodigious guitarist he claimed to be. So from all accounts, Garrit Flant was indeed an undisputed superstar. But after just five years of performing, and to his fans' dismay, he retired with short notice and vanished into an obscure life in rural Scotland. Then, his name had popped up in the news recently because the Rock & Roll Hall of Fame had announced an award for his years-old single, "Happy Flappy Girl," as an important influence on the art form. Rock wasn't Peppa's thing, but she knew the song well because Whitney had covered it, making it an international hit.

Now the hangdog seemed to have recovered enough for Peppa to thread her arm through his and whisk him around the maze of corridors. When they entered the office, GoGo immediately re-embraced his inner imp. Ignoring Ivan's attempt to shake hands, he began to prowl the room, testing the cushions on furniture with his palm, running his fingers across the tops of artwork, checking for dust. He picked up a package of macadamia nuts, shook it as if assessing its quantity, then tossed it back. While GoGo continued these antics, Ivan backed himself against a wall with an expression Peppa had never seen before—something akin to fear.

Eventually GoGo applied his brakes and stood in the middle of the room. "This office reminds me of the day I saw the Pyramids for the first time. *Beige.*" He pointed to the west-facing window. "Newark, New Jersey. Home of a highly dysfunctional airport. But superb Portuguese food, I've heard." Then he pivoted his finger in the opposite direction. "And *you* must be the much-lauded Ivan Scherbo. Native of Belarus. Noted for its sweets during Stalin's time and endless recipes calling for overcooked potatoes. No doubt you're thrilled to be in the US."

"Yes, yes. I mean, I like the States. Quite a lot," Ivan stuttered.

"Speaking of ancestral lands, I'd like to share a factoid surely not discovered in your research, which I presume has been copious."

"We've certainly done our homework as we do for all our clients," Ivan said. "I hope that doesn't bother you."

"On the contrary. I'm comforted that you made the effort, pending what you've unearthed, of course. But about the factoid. Ironically, it involves, in a roundabout fashion, your homeland. My great-great-grandfather lived in Minsk his entire life."

"Is that so?"

"It is," GoGo affirmed. "But here's the roundabout part. According to family lore, the Flants are direct descendants of Pepin the Short. But exactly how, or even *if*, the King of the Franks wandered so far east as to impregnate a young lass, which eventually produced the likes of me, has been a controversial topic."

"But it was centuries ago . . . why the worry?" Ivan asked.

"Well, if proven to be true, and objectively I can't say I'd object, it would give me quite the glow of royalty. Which is *exactly* the kind of fodder the tabloids would love to sink their teeth into and malign me by claiming that it's *not* true. Birtherism at its worst. Meanwhile, I'm just trying to live a humble life in total obscurity. So, I felt it wise to preemptively entrust this potential bombshell to you, and of course the ever-discreet Penelope."

"Communication in this office is strictly confidential."

"My new and trusted friend. You may call me GoGo."

Ivan frowned. "How's that? I don't understand you."

"Am I speaking Russian? It's quite simple. All my intimates call me Go. *Go.* Penelope and I have already conducted the sort of exchange which has rendered us familiar. Do join my exclusive club." He stood up and launched into his House of Windsor act with another gravity-defying curtsy.

"Please. Mr. Flant—I mean, GoGo. That isn't necessary."

"It's known as the Balmoral dip. Come. I'll teach you." GoGo reached out a hand, and Ivan immediately recoiled. "A bit fidgety, are we? Okay, I've a better idea. Penelope, let's you and I perform a jig. Dancing cheers me so."

Dancing is, utterly, the entertainment of last resort.

"No. I mean . . . I can't."

"Surely you learned this staple of Irish foot-flopping in your formative years. It can't be far from the dreadful clogging I was forced to commit to memory at parochial school. The nuns? *Beasts.*"

"I'm afraid I never learned to dance. I've been told I lack coordination."

"You don't *look* like a galumpher, though only God knows what's under that gunnysack of a dress. But I'll take your word for it."

"Also, we really should start the meeting," Peppa suggested.

"What a mature alternative! Let's sit on this uncomfortable-looking sofa. I'll need you in the middle, my dear." He pointed to the gap where the two cushions met.

"Ivan prefers me in that chair," she said, indicating her usual seat.

"Oh, pish-posh. Everyone knows that communication between two men always has a better outcome with a woman between them. *Literally*." He jabbed toward the sofa with his chin. "Sit."

Peppa straddled herself across the two cushions, and Ivan tentatively lowered himself to her left, wedging his body as close to the armrest as possible. GoGo saturated every inch to her right, so much so that his body mashed against hers. She could smell his breath—sweet and slightly smoky from the Indian meal on the flight over. His body heat, particularly intense, seemed to penetrate the fabric of her dress and spread across her skin.

Collapse. Oh, collapse into all that you cannot control, because fate is simply the truth and one must, in the end, submit.

As peculiar as the situation was, Peppa was relieved, because it seemed that Virginia believed in fate, after all. So she angled a few more degrees toward GoGo. He nodded as if thanking her. Then, he wedged his face into the crook of her neck and began to sob. Peppa wanted to comfort him but was unsure what was appropriate. She defaulted to remaining very still, figuring that no reaction would likely help whatever had come over him to pass more quickly. And it worked, because in less than a minute, GoGo sat up and pried a crumpled hanky from his jumpsuit sleeve to blot tears.

"Forgive me," he croaked.

"Do you feel better now?" Peppa asked.

"I can't say. But I'm grateful that you allowed me to invade the tender area between your chin and clavicle. It's a gift to remember what safety feels like. Ivan, don't let this girl get away from you."

"I've no plans," Ivan murmured.

"But, oh, I'm such a *fool*," GoGo moaned.

"Why? You just had a . . . moment," Peppa said.

"But I went on and on about . . . nothing. You can throw me out as you wish. I'll wander. Aimlessly."

"Don't be silly," she said.

"But I've *wept*."

"Perfectly normal."

"That simply can't *be*."

"It's true," Peppa said. "People cry in this office all the time. Look, we should go ahead with the meeting. Ivan's blocked out the entire morning. And he's a master. You'll see."

The meeting began. Ivan probed and GoGo, no surprise, resisted. They bandied back and forth like this for some time, trying to find that liminal position both could relax into. And when GoGo eventually unleashed his story, it became clear that it would take all of Ivan's skill to dig him out of his financial troubles. But toward the end, when Peppa caught Ivan's glance and his eyebrow popped up, she immediately knew that they had come to the same conclusion. Money was not GoGo's real problem.

Peppa and Ivan were late for their reservation at The Shell. And since only three lobsters remained in the tank, the hostess quickly escorted them to what was now their usual out-of-the-way booth near the kitchen entrance. Ivan nabbed their waiter, reserved the lobsters, whatever their gender and weight, and then downed an entire glass of mineral water in several gigantic gulps.

"That was a very strange story," he said.

"It sounds to me like out-and-out theft, Ivan. Shouldn't the police be called?"

"I think not. They've been common-law partners for years. I doubt a charge like that would gain traction. In any case, the illegal transfers occurred in the UK, so New York wouldn't have jurisdiction."

"But GoGo has triple citizenship," Peppa said. "England, Scotland, and the US."

"How'd you find that out?"

"It's on that new Wikipedia site. His bio. Reviews. Performance stats."

"Good to know about the residency aspect because it'll make things easier when we start to sell off his properties in the States. I've already determined that they're substantial enough that even with a sizable kill fee to the boyfriend, beyond what's already been stolen, GoGo will regroup nicely. It'll take time, that's all. More worrisome is his mental state."

"It's hard to imagine someone like GoGo putting up with that kind of emotional abuse, and for so many years," Peppa said.

"I know. The boyfriend really had his number."

"I was surprised that you offered for him to stay at your place tonight."

"It wasn't one of my better moves. But by the end, he was so incoherent I truly felt it unwise to leave him in a hotel room by himself. I don't think he's actually suicidal, but he's the sort who might try as a cry for help. In the moment, it just seemed like an expedient option."

"I guess better to be safe. I assume you have plenty of room?"

Ivan chuckled. "More than enough. Even for the likes of GoGo."

"You're in one of those silos over by the river, right?"

"I am."

"My dad hates them. Says they're a blight. Do you mind if I ask your square footage?"

"Just over three thousand."

"For one person? Sorry, but that's pretty ridiculous," Peppa said.

"I know. But it was a fluke, really. I bought it from a client who signed on with a ton of debt—totally underwater. The real estate market was depressed at the time, and he wasn't able to wait for an upswing. Our strategy was to use my purchase money to rebuild his portfolio. I admit to lowballing him, but he wasn't in any position to argue. We worked the whole thing on a handshake. No brokers. All in all, a sweet deal."

"Nifty. And you must have spectacular views."

"Funny you should say. I don't look out the windows much at all. And I use less than half the space. There's an entire wing with a separate entrance I offer to friends visiting from Europe. It's been useful in that way."

"So, GoGo will stay in that section?" she asked.

"Right. I instructed my building to admit him through that entrance. The thing is, it's been a year since anyone's visited, and I can't remember if the door connecting the two spaces is locked." Ivan paused, giving her a tight smile. "GoGo will snoop."

"I can see that."

"Damn. I must be losing it. Peppa, would you mind coming to the apartment after work? Help me deal with him? I have a sinking feeling he's going to try to stay longer than one night. I know it's an imposition, but he obviously responds to you. In fact, you put all my clients at ease. Whenever I'm on the phone with them, they always ask after you."

"But I don't say a word during the transcriptions. And a minimum at the elevator."

"It's your aura," he said with a wink.

"I doubt that. Anyway, staying even one night is already unusual, so it's hard to imagine GoGo'd try for more."

"I know that, and you know that. But who the hell knows *what* GoGo knows. He's lived a king's life. He's used to getting what he wants. And he's . . . unpredictable. You'll help?"

"Of course."

While the waiter dropped the lobsters and bibbed them up, Peppa further mulled over Ivan's concerns. "I've got an idea. Let's have dinner catered in tonight. Something really fancy."

"Like a seduction?"

"Exactly."

"This is good. He adores being fussed over. And he clearly loves food. *That's* obvious enough." Ivan smirked.

"Don't fat-shame! I'm sure he's got issues."

"Sorry. What I mean is, we'll get him happy. Or at least agreeable."

"Then we'll ease him into the idea of a hotel."

"Peppa, you're brilliant."

"Which restaurant?" she asked.

"Gramercy Tavern. I know Danny Meyer. He's the owner. Drop my name. They'll pay more attention to the order."

By this time, they'd finished the meal and tidied themselves with damp towels. Peppa had just taken her first sip of cappuccino when she remembered what they were really supposed to be discussing . . . or celebrating. "I want more details on my toilet boys."

"I'd rather you tell me what happened this morning. The reason you were late."

"Oh, that. I have to go on a date. An Irish plumber."

"You *have* to?"

"I promised."

"Peppa, you're an adult. You don't have to do this."

"I kind of do."

"But who you date is private. Maybe it's not my place, but your parents shouldn't be involved. And can't they see how you're thriving?"

"I stopped telling them anything after my first week of work."

"You're not seeing this clearly."

"Ivan, please . . ."

"They don't appreciate your talents. Your potential."

Peppa slumped in her chair. She watched two waiters round a corner from opposite directions and almost collide. Someone in the kitchen yelled, "*Pick up!*" four times in less than ten seconds. A side exit door opened and a crate of lettuce was tossed into the corridor. How could all this chaos come together to produce beautifully plated food? Unless you worked in a restaurant, this was, just like her life, a complicated thing to explain.

"What?" Ivan prodded.

"They expected me to join the business. Eventually take over. And that's off the table now. I've forced a situation where they're going to have to reevaluate and make some big adjustments. Work more years than they'd intended. Their life hasn't been easy. And . . . I'm really worried about my mom."

"Why? You've never talked about her."

We don't choose any given moment. It appears, and if we don't act, the loss can be irrevocable.

"She's sick . . . actually, my mom has a mental illness," Peppa said.

"Really. Wanna tell me?"

"Oh, there's just so much, but I'll make it short. She sleeps a lot. Or not at all. She rarely goes out of the house. But sometimes she does. Then she wanders. And gets . . . lost. When I was younger, I didn't know. My mom was just my mom. But once I understood, my dad and I teamed up, trying to keep her safe. Mostly from herself. We've had terrible times, Ivan. And now I feel so guilty because since I've started this job, neither is doing well. Even my dad is quietly freaking out. And when I tell them I'm moving out, it's going to be really, really bad. So going on this date is the least I can do. This one last thing."

"I'm glad you told me. I'll do anything I can to help."

He meant well. But at the edge of her mind, Peppa knew that one way or another, she was going to ruin everything for her parents. And no one, no one in the world, could do a thing to help prevent that.

"Let's go," she said with an upbeat smile. "We've got that Floridian flying in."

"Right. Mr. Palm Beach."

She plucked at the fabric of her dress, aware of the meal in her belly. "I'm such a blob."

"You look absolutely wonderful, Peppa."

THE VIEW FROM A ROOM

WHEN IVAN OPENED THE DOOR TO HIS APARTMENT AND PEPPA STEPPED INSIDE, all that registered were faint lights sprinkled in front of her. Then within a few seconds, she saw an enormous window spanning the entire wall and realized those lights were stars emerging out of the dusk. And this was the impressive view of the Hudson River that Ivan professed never to pay any attention to. He turned a switch, and a floor lamp did its best to illuminate the largest living room Peppa had ever set foot in. The shade, made from cut glass in every color, represented an idealized version of dragonflies. A curlicue wooden-framed sofa with button-tufted black velvet fabric on both seat and back faced the view. She looked around, confirming that the rest of the room was, indeed, empty. Even so, the sofa and the lamp looked as if they were meant to be a couple.

"I like your style," she said, plopping onto the sofa.

"What style? I scavenged this stuff at a flea market in Dumbo a few months ago. Before that—well, since I moved in—there's been literally nothing here."

"You thought you were just throwing it together, but choices were made."

"Maybe. But the sofa was in decent shape and the lamp had been rewired, so I grabbed them."

She pushed herself off the sofa and joined Ivan, who was now staring out the window.

"Not bad," she said, pointing to the view.

"It's nice, I suppose."

"When's the last time you looked?"

"What do you mean?"

"At lunch you said you didn't look out the window."

"A long time. I'm pretty fried when I get home, so it's straight to the kitchen for a meal and then off to the bedroom. And I don't think I've sat on this flouncy thing more than a dozen times," he said, gesturing at the sofa. "It's embarrassing, but this living room's sole function has been as a very expensive passageway."

"So, what happened?" she asked.

"Um . . . too busy?"

"For five years?"

"I know. It's sad. But this rummage is a start, right?"

"In another five I'll expect a rug. And if you can manage to really stretch out, try for a coffee table too."

"If I can't meet that deadline, I'm in deep trouble."

She noticed a hallway entrance at one end of the living room. "GoGo's in there?"

"Uh-huh. There's a heavy door at the very end of that hallway, so he can't hear us. But let me show you the kitchen first."

Peppa was heartened to find the kitchen thoroughly lived in, smelling simultaneously of something baked and something sautéed. The walls looked like mustard, the cabinets a sweet blue. A steel table long enough to seat eight occupied a bay at a north-facing window, and she could just make out the spires of a church in the distance. At the other end of the room, a professional chef's oven and a six-burner cooktop snuggled between black stone counters. Ivan roamed the room, repositioning gadgets to make space on the counters. An elite espresso/cappuccino maker, a fancy rice cooker, a blender/juicer combo. Even the same brand of slow cooker her mom rarely used but insisted should stay on the counter in the unlikely event that she got inspired before noon. Peppa ran her hand across a counter surface, gathering a residue of flour into her palm.

"You actually use all this stuff?" she asked, clapping white dust into the sink.

"Of course. I cook on the weekends to prepare dinners for the coming week." Ivan opened the Sub-Zero doors to display a lineup of plastic containers, all carefully labeled.

She stooped down. "Calamari—Lidia; lamb chops—Bobby; stuffed chicken breasts—Jacques. I have no clue who any of these people are."

"Famous chefs. Jacques Pépin is my god. His deboning technique is unparalleled. You haven't lived until you've tasted his stuffed breasts." Ivan pulled the container out, removed the lid, and stared at the food as if waiting for the bird to thank him for the compliment. "See the spinach poking out? You blend it with ricotta cheese and one egg as a binder. Sea salt and cilantro. Food is important to me."

"*Really*. I'd never have guessed," she said, laughing.

"Hey, I'm serious!" He pointed to cookbooks lining shelves on either side of the bay window. "They're not just eye candy. Most nights, I'm up late studying recipes and planning meals."

"So, why'd we bother ordering in? There're half a dozen fancy dinners sitting in the fridge, and I'm assuming they're all really good."

"We've known him less than a day, but I can't imagine GoGo eating a reheated dinner, no matter how delicious. He'd go off the rails. But let's get the table ready before we see what mischief he's been up to."

Ivan took plates and glassware from upper cabinets, and she found knives and forks and striped placemats with matching napkins in various drawers. They laid out three settings at one end and piled two weeks' worth of newspapers into a neat stack at the other. She spied a cluster of wine bottles sitting on the floor in a corner and grabbed one.

"What do you think?" she asked, displaying a Pinot Noir.

"What are we eating?"

"Danny Meyer insisted on steak."

"The Pinot's too light. Merlot is better. The wine pantry is around the corner. There's a 1949 from Argentina that I particularly like. They're arranged alphabetically by country, so look to the left and it should be on the top rack."

The "pantry" happened to be a high-tech temperature-controlled room with gauges and needles straight out of NASA. Peppa estimated a thousand bottles but easily located the exact Merlot he wanted. She pulled sparkling water from the fridge, set that and the wine on the table, then surveyed the scene. A large red clay bowl stuck haphazardly at the top of the refrigerator caught her attention. She took it down and, after wiping dust and dead gnats from the bottom of the vessel, placed it in the middle of the table as a centerpiece.

"This okay?" she asked.

"Sure. One of my anthropology professors at Oxford made it and gave it to me."

"It's stunning."

"I've always carried this piece wherever I've lived. She was a scholar and excavator of centuries-old ruins all over Belarus. That's how we became close—my country. She used to try to pick my brain about the culture, but I can't say I had much to tell her, because I left at such a young age." He picked up the bowl and rubbed his fingers against the incised surface. "These are her reinterpretation of petroglyphs." He placed it back on the table and rotated the vessel so the main decoration faced the entrance to the kitchen.

"How did you have time for anthropology?" Peppa asked. "You were a finance major, I assume."

"I took a double major—anthropology, and I read classics. I never got a degree in finance, but I did need to make money. The job at LBS fell into my lap through word of mouth."

"What luck you've had."

"I guess," Ivan said. "But as it turns out, I am good with numbers and understanding trends and economic forces. It's not rocket science. Actually, it's a bit of a one-armed bandit."

"Gambling?"

"Yep. At least, the stock market is. But don't you ever tell anybody I said that."

"No way. You're my meal ticket."

He laughed and then immediately turned sober. "I guess the witching hour is here. Time to fetch GoGo." But instead of leading the way out of the kitchen, Ivan pulled out a chair, sat with a thump and thrummed his fingers. He plucked a piece of lint off his jacket sleeve, watched it drift to the floor, and groaned. "Dear *God*."

"What?"

"GoGo staying here. It's all wrong."

"You mean like against company policy?" she asked, taking a seat opposite him.

"Not that I know of. I mean, there's no impropriety. I just can't believe I offered."

"You had a good reason at the time."

"Yeah, he was miserable," Ivan agreed. "But it's something more—he's like a very charming hysteric. And crafty. I bet he's manipulated a million people into getting what he wants. Look what happened today. I *never* have dinner guests and within the course of one meeting, he's not only eating here, but he's sleeping here too. This is completely out of character for me. I feel like his latest dupe."

"Hold on. I called some five-star hotels with great restaurants. They have vacancies. He can have his pick."

"Sounds nice on paper, but do you really think he'll leave without making a scene? You saw how unhinged he got this morning."

"Well, he's not crazy . . . I mean, not exactly. Just an oddball," she said.

"Crazy is doable. In a way, obvious. Oddballs can be much more difficult."

"Look, if he balks at the hotel idea, let's have a plan B. Make something up. Like . . . your mother's coming for a visit tomorrow."

"Nope. She's dead."

"Oh, I'm sorry."

"No, no. What I mean is, he'll see the lie in my face. His BS detector is on hyper-alert-autopilot. Most clients *want* to believe everything I say."

Peppa wondered what was happening to her self-assured boss, who was usually impervious to the whims of privileged clients. He always knew how to handle every tantrum and ward off even the slightest glitch. And now she saw that look again—fear.

An attempt to assist another in distress might also, in an oblique way, mitigate one's own seemingly endless drifting and sinking.

Peppa thought, *It's worth a try*.

"How about this?" she said. "We tell him the building needs access to his section tomorrow morning because a leak's been discovered in the apartment below."

Ivan sat up straight and nodded half a dozen times. "Good. This has potential. Give me more," he said, prompting her with his hands.

"Okay, let's see. We could say it was discovered just yesterday. And . . . the people below don't use that section much either. So . . . when the cleaning lady went in for her once-a-month dust-up, she found a mess. The problem would likely be in the pipes behind the walls, and they've called a plumber for tomorrow morning. Ergo . . . GoGo has no choice but to leave."

"Excellent. You're way too good at this."

"You think?"

"Uh-huh. That's why *you'll* have to tell him," Ivan said.

"*Me? Oh* no."

"This is your field. You know construction. You'll be able to outthink him. Back him into a corner. You can do it, Peppa. I know you can. He'll agree to whatever you say. He adores you!"

"Ivan, don't you think you're overreacting just a tad?"

"Absolutely not. As I said before, he's an eccentric. Unpredictable. And ridiculous. That outfit? My God, Karl Lagerfeld could sue him for image infringement."

"Who's *that*?"

"There're stacks of *Vogue* in the kitchen pantry. I'll show you a picture later if you want. But seriously. Peppa. I need you to take charge."

"Okay, okay. I'll bring it up at dinner. No, better during dessert. I've ordered blueberry tarts. Danny Meyer said they have a new pastry chef and it's the best dessert in the city. Is he famous?"

"Yes. In the restaurant world, really famous. Also, he dresses well."

They walked down the long hallway off the living room and passed two empty bedrooms, and then a third with a large sleigh bed and other spare furnishings that was obviously Ivan's. Ivan found the door separating the two sections locked and looked at Peppa, mouthing *Thank God*. The guest section opened directly into a living room filled with granny-like furniture. Red and gold striped wallpaper crowded the walls. Heavy drapery panels at the windows swooped with thick rope tiebacks. The ceiling had been painted red with a glossy finish. The TV, turned to CNN but on mute, was mounted amid wall-to-wall bookshelves surrounded by fussy molding. Peppa turned around a few times, taking in the entirety of the room, unable to disguise her disapproval.

"Pretty dreadful, isn't it?" he said. "A leftover from the former owner. I haven't found the motivation to redo it."

"For a second, I was worried you had some hand in this horror. No wonder you never use this part of the apartment. But I'm curious what GoGo thinks."

"I'll guarantee he can't get enough of this dated, over-the-top nonsense. His castle in Scotland would probably make the top-ten list of rock and roll homes guaranteed to cause indigestion due to bad taste."

"That is just plain mean," Peppa said.

"I know."

Off the living room, a small but efficiently designed kitchen smelled of garlic and fried rice. Ivan opened the refrigerator to find Chinese takeout bins littering the shelves.

"Well, well. Seems he's managed a meal in spite of his woes," he said.

"Everybody has to eat."

"Sure, but nine cartons?"

Peppa leveled her eyes at him. "Don't judge."

"Sorry."

The kitchen table was strewn with newspapers—the *Post*, *Daily News*, and *The Times*. Each had been opened to the crossword puzzle.

"Look, Ivan. They're all completed—and in pen. GoGo may be a nut, but he's smart."

"It's a skill, not an indication of intelligence."

"But you need a good vocabulary and knowledge of lots of subjects, like current events and history. Trivia for sure."

"It's a trick. Means nothing."

"Can *you* do that?"

Ivan paused. "No. But are these answers even right? For all we know, he could have filled in the squares with random letters."

"Why would he do something like that?"

"That's what narcissists do."

"And your point is?" Peppa asked.

"He'd do it to impress *himself*."

"That's just ridiculous."

"Well . . . true. But he does have excellent penmanship. I'll give him that."

The tub in the bathroom glistened with droplets from recent use. A Kate Spade toiletry bag was zippered closed—no sign of a toothbrush, razor, or other personal items had been left out. Even the toilet seat and lid were in the down position.

"He's a neat freak," she noted.

"I'm in shock."

"Will you give the guy a break? Stop inventing reasons to dislike him. He'll be gone in the morning."

"Your lips to God's—"

"Wait. Listen, Ivan."

Oh, Danny boy, the pipes, the pipes are calling
From glen to glen, and down the mountainside.

The summer's gone, and all the flowers are falling,
It's you, it's you must go and I must bide.

"He's got a true high tenor," Peppa whispered.

"So? He can sing like a girl. Big deal."

"My God. Will you just quit it?"

"I'll try," Ivan said.

"Wait, here it comes . . . the high note."

It's I'll be heeeeeeeere, in sunshine or in shadow,
Oh Danny boy, oh Danny boy, I love . . . you . . . so!

"That's the end." Peppa pointed to the door. "Go in."

"You first."

"What if he's not dressed?"

"I can't look at *that*."

"You think *I* should?"

"Hallllloooo!" GoGo yodeled from the bedroom.

They found him lying diagonally across the bed on his back, wrapped in a black silk robe with a gold sash knotted at the top of his belly. And for some reason, he'd covered his hairless head with a towel turban. Now he performed a surprisingly agile scissor kick with his legs, exposing purple pajamas underneath the robe.

"I heard you both yakking out there," he said. "See? I'm thoroughly decent. And clean. I've had a long soak in a marginally large tub. Oiled my cuticles. Slept in bits and pieces, interspersed with several weeping jags. And you'll be comforted to know that New York City's Chinese takeaway is still the best."

"Your 'Danny Boy' was absolutely beautiful," Peppa said.

"Wasn't it? I developed my vocal chops at the paws of, not surprisingly, the nuns. They heard me singing in the shower one day and tossed me to the choir. The rest is rock and roll history. But enough of memory's dirt road. A thorough bath ritual always renews my appetite. I trust there's something divine in store for dinner?"

"Steak," Peppa said.

"I was just thinking of Kerry cows on the glen before you came in. What a gloriously intuitive human you are."

He rolled off the bed, ripped the turban from his head, then slipped into a pair of beaded slippers. They proceeded down the hallway single file and entered the living room. GoGo headed straight for the window while Peppa and Ivan sat on the sofa. After swiveling south to north several times, he reeled around and planted himself directly in front of Ivan.

Ivan winced. "Yes, GoGo?"

"I want you to know I tried very hard not to be offended by the *locked door* I encountered earlier in the day. No doubt you instructed the building staff to secure the place before I arrived. After all, you couldn't very well have an emotionally over-wrought *Brit* running amok."

"That's not it at all," Ivan said. "That section is meant for visiting guests, which I haven't had for many months. I had no idea it was locked. Please, don't take it personally."

"I take *every*thing personally."

"Yes, I'm beginning to see that."

"In any case," GoGo continued, "my curiosity was really quite innocent. I've never been in one of these unattractive steel tubes before and wanted to determine for myself if they are, in fact, the disasters so many speak about. Now that I see the place, even in almost pitch dark, the interior construction is thoroughly substandard. And other than this knockoff Tiffany lamp and utterly sad Duncan Phyfe reproduction sofa, might I ask what you're trying to prove with this empty room? I can feel the implied hostility."

"GoGo, please," Peppa said. "You're a guest in Ivan's home."

"Yes, I know. He invited me."

"But are you aware of how unusual that is?" she asked.

He patted the lapels of his robe and re-tightened the sash. "Well. I suppose. Forgive me. It's just that I've been frantic with jet lag and overwhelmed with my disastrous personal life and the impending gutting of my finances. But I *am* grateful for the lodgings, which are one hundred percent . . . adequate. Thank goodness I packed for a month."

Horror brushed across Ivan's face. He mouthed to Peppa, *Help.*

"Um . . . the meal will be here any minute," Peppa said, motioning to the entrance door. "*Right*, Ivan?"

"Oh . . . yes . . . I'll meet it in the lobby. The doorman sometimes takes his time to buzz."

Peppa patted the cushion next to her. GoGo pranced over, kicked off his slippers, and lay down, placing his feet in her lap. Both big toes had disturbingly large bunions. She draped a chenille throw over his feet.

"I know," he said with a sigh. "They're hideous."

"They're not. It's just chilly in here."

"I've always considered cold rooms a passive method of torture. We'd never find the thermostat because this place has no lighting. And even if we did find it, Ivan's probably got it under lock and key."

"Why are you so irritated with Ivan?" she asked.

"He doesn't like me. And he judges me."

"That's not true. Not exactly. Ivan is just a reserved person. Can't you give him a break?"

"Maybe, but all I know is, thin gay men dressed in Tom Ford suits look down their noses at overweight gay men in Lagerfeld. At least that's been my experience. My beastly ex-boyfriend Sebastian being exemplar numero uno. He's skinny too."

She waved away the comment. "Ivan's not gay."

"Peppa. It takes a gay to know a gay."

"I really don't think so, GoGo."

"Has he ever mentioned a social life? Even once?"

"Um . . . no."

"Classic. It's likely he's not out to his company. But trust me, that man's best friend is a disco ball."

Just then, Ivan re-entered the apartment with the dinner boxes stacked in his arms. "Let's eat," was all Peppa could think to say.

The food had retained a good amount of heat during transit, so while she and GoGo took their seats, Ivan plated directly. He chewed with deliberation, savoring the distinct seasonings, taking his time between mouthfuls of steak, peppered mashed potatoes, and garlicky string beans. GoGo, on the other hand, gobbled nonstop, smacking his lips when some flavor seemed to strike him as particularly deserving. Peppa ate only the steak. She found the potatoes and beans to be so over-seasoned with all that pepper and garlic, it didn't much matter what the food was underneath. And, still enthralled with her newfound love of seafood, Peppa would have much preferred shrimp to start, then scallops for the main course.

Leonard reports that seashells are the remains of strange, meaty creatures who live an innocuous existence. But oh, the exquisite beauty of their abandoned husks.

Oh, Virginia, Peppa thought, *why? Why that memory? And why now?*

But it was in her head, so Peppa had no choice but to recall that bitter-cold Christmas morning, when her mom had bundled her in a new red coat from Santa Claus, and they walked the dozen blocks to the beach entrance. They played a game—seeing who could fill a pail of seashells the fastest. And that was fun. Her mom even laughed. Then, Peppa, who was at this point quite cold, asked if they could go home. Her mom's mood changed instantly, and she threw all the seashells into the surf. They couldn't leave until they found more perfect seashells. After examining every shell and eliminating those with even the smallest flaw, Peppa managed to fill half the pail. But her mom tossed those too, because now the seashells needed to be bigger than a dime and smaller than a quarter. Peppa didn't know what that meant—she was only six years old, after all. But she guessed at the size and presented a single shell. Her mom threw it at Peppa. Then the memory got fuzzy—mostly impressions and sensations. Sitting on a bench with her mom, who was now crying. A burning in her toes and fingers from the cold. And then, the great relief when she no longer felt anything at all.

"This meal was nothing less than a triumph," GoGo declared, pushing himself back from the table.

"Gramercy Tavern has steak down to perfection," Ivan confirmed, tipping the last of his wine. "And we've got tarts for dessert. Blueberry."

"Scottish blueberries are an abomination, so I'm most eager to be overwhelmed," GoGo said.

Ivan gave the tarts a light dusting of confectioners' sugar. After placing three servings on the table, he picked up a pair of binoculars from the windowsill, turned his back on them, and began spying on the state of New Jersey.

Peppa figured this was her cue. "GoGo. May I ask what your plans are?"

"My plans?" He'd devoured his entire tart in three quick bites and was now eyeing Ivan's.

"You mentioned at the office that you intend to remain in New York for the time being," she said. "We were wondering what you had in mind. In terms of a living situation."

"This place will suffice. I could do with a larger bathroom. Sheets with a minimum five hundred thread count would be nice too. But as they say, the one who begs cannot always be the one who chooses."

Ivan coughed and pivoted north toward the church.

"I don't think Ivan can accommodate you for more than one night," Peppa said.

"But not twenty minutes ago he said those quarters have been vacant for ages. *Must* I beg?"

"Of course not. But we've actually thought of a much better situation for you. Especially since you appreciate great food. There're a number of hotels with really fine restaurants. You'd have 24/7 room service and every amenity. We'll get you settled into one in the morning."

"It wouldn't work," GoGo said.

Ivan veered south toward the Trade Towers.

"They're first rate—" she said.

"I'm sure they are, but that's not the point."

"Then what?"

"My mental state. I'm literally at my limit."

Ivan aimed at the moon.

"And I simply cannot risk the exposure," GoGo said.

"Exposure?" Peppa said.

"In a word, *headlines*."

"I really don't follow."

"If I stay at a hotel, it'll get out to the press on hour number one of day number two."

"But you haven't performed in years. No offense, GoGo, but do you really think where you're staying is newsworthy?"

"Dear girl. You've obviously been living in the middle of the ocean on an island called *Tabloid Exile*. *Everything* about me is newsworthy, including taking out the garbage, not that I would ever perform such a chore. Why do you think I've secluded myself all these years? And to put a finer point on it, I'm not exactly Cary Grant."

"Meaning?"

"Goodness me. If you weren't so charming and smart and I didn't already adore you as much as I do, I might interpret your naïveté as a consequence of being left in the birth canal too long." He grabbed Ivan's untouched tart, took a huge bite, and returned the remainder. "You don't actually believe I was the embodiment of Sebastian's fantasy. Wealth and especially my fame were what he was after. I knew it, and the rags who felt it their duty to remind the entire world at least once a month knew it. In any case, he *was* lovey-dovey for a good number of years, until his inner brute showed up. The insults. The gaslighting. The *spitting*. It was like the worst D movie ever imagined. Kind of like Susan Hayward in *I Want to Live* meets Patty Duke in *Valley of the Dolls*. And do either of you even know these movie references?"

"Nope," Peppa said.

"I'm from Belarus, remember?" Ivan said, without taking the binoculars from his eyes.

"Well, Susan's locked up in a women's prison filled with all manner of deviants, and Patty's a washed-up drug-addicted movie star—"

"We don't need the story," Peppa said.

"Okay, fine," GoGo said. "But first I should fill you in on some details I neglected to disclose earlier in the day. And they'll undoubtedly impact whatever financial shenanigans Ivan means to accomplish."

Ivan turned the binoculars directly on GoGo. "I'm listening."

"*Now* he's interested."

"Proceed," Peppa said.

"Well, I don't mind paying the little bugger off. But he's boarded himself up in *my* castle. I've left behind everything that means anything to me. My pride and joy, a candy apple red 1966 Fender Stratocaster. Four Tiffany lamps. *Real* ones. A couple of early Francis Bacon oils. My treasured, very small, J. M. W. Turner watercolor. But the worst is, he's sold off my gigantic collection of Lagerfeld haute couture men's clothing. Gone. Auf Wiedersehen. I hope you're listening, Ivan, because—"

"GoGo!" Peppa said with exasperation. "I'm still unclear as to exactly why you can't stay in a hotel."

"My dear girl. One day you'll understand that the world would be ever so dull if we were forced to cease discussing the ephemera of our lives simply for purposes of *expediency*. That said, the paparazzi will, and in the most vicious manner possible, pounce. At which point the hotel will *eject* me. Then my life will enter a terribly muddled phase, consisting of long flights and less-than-optimal living quarters. And now that I am facing potential homelessness, thanks to Ivan, I have a sudden urge to eat something. To wit, I am once again famished."

Ivan returned the binoculars to the window ledge and plopped into the seat at the opposite end of the table. "Help yourself to whatever's in the fridge."

GoGo heaved himself up and threw open both doors. "Haaalllooo! What have we here? Jacques? Julia?"

"Ivan cooks," Peppa said.

"Does he now?"

"I do," Ivan confirmed.

GoGo pulled out one container from the bottom of the stack. "Hmm. Eric. As in Eric *Ripert*? I'm lunching at Le Bernardin later in the week. He's introducing me to this Tony Bourdain fellow. Says he's an absolute darling. Wrote a restaurant warts-and-all book everyone's been on about." He opened the container and sniffed. "Is this the cold poached salmon from Eric's cookbook?"

"It is," Ivan said.

"Mind if I take a bite?"

"I wouldn't dare stop you."

GoGo consumed the entire meal in less than a minute.

"Well? What do you think?" Ivan asked.

GoGo looked toward the ceiling and rimmed his lips with his tongue. "You've captured exactly the correct balance of herbs without obliterating the essence of the fish. After all, a fish must always, in the end, remain a fish."

"You're not just saying that?"

"Ivan. You've known me less than twelve hours. But do I seem like someone who holds back the truth under any circumstance?"

"I suppose not. But do you really know Eric Ripert?"

"He's been to my castle numerous times. We bonded when I met him at La Tour d'Argent in Paris. I predicted his rise from the beginning."

"You're joking."

"Ivan. When I crack a joke, you'll know it. You'll know it because you'll laugh. Most likely with a joy you've rarely experienced."

"Eric's my god . . . after Jacques, that is."

GoGo smiled impishly.

"You know him *too*?"

"If I ever manage to father a child, admittedly a remote possibility, Jacques has agreed to be the wee one's godfather."

"I see," Ivan said, looking chastened.

"Do you? I may have stuffed myself into a castle in Scotland, but I've led a full and fascinating life. All of which has been difficult to accomplish for a million and two reasons. So, at this moment, I believe applause may be in order. However, I'll settle for staying in your enormous, albeit sad, apartment. Hotel *indeed*. The very thought!"

With GoGo resurrecting his indignation, Peppa felt the moment had arrived for plan B. "There's actually a problem which is out of Ivan's control."

"What could possibly be out of his control?" GoGo asked. "He owns this dreadful place."

"It's the plumbing," she said.

"I took a bath. Water arrived and exited. Everything seemed in order."

"Not on this floor. It's the apartment below—"

"My life is in tatters and you're talking about pipes in a far-off land called the *apartment below*?"

"It's more complicated than that because, see, the cleaning lady downstairs, well, she was dusting, and—"

"Hold on, Peppa," Ivan said. "I saw the super in the lobby. It seems the problem has been resolved. GoGo, you're welcome to stay."

GoGo's face lit up. "Oh, we'll have such a time of it, Ivan. You'll cook and I'll . . . eat!"

Peppa grabbed the binoculars, walked to the farthest window possible, and focused on the northernmost view. She listened as they compared notes on the best restaurants in Paris and Berlin, and some place called Malmö. They debated whether someone called Anna Wintour, twelve years in at *Vogue*, was proving a worthy successor to another she didn't know of, Grace Mirabella. They commiserated about how much they missed Diana Vreeland—and who was that? She heard them migrate to the fridge to inspect and discuss every dish Ivan had prepared. Then, GoGo invited Ivan to join him for lunch at Le Bernardin and meet Eric Ripert.

There are those moments that we pray would vanish from our brains; so as to recalibrate, or to roll back. That is, to wipe out the memory so that we might live another day.

That would be just wonderful, Virginia.

Peppa returned the binoculars to the window ledge, skirted around the table, and headed toward the kitchen door. The Friday afternoon rush to the Hamptons would be over by now, so she could easily snare a cab. And during the ride home, she'd refine all the ways she meant to eviscerate the Irish plumber on Sunday morning. Or maybe she'd just cancel him and every other hope she held about her future.

Dear Virginia, she thought, *why didn't you warn me?*

"Hey, Missy Dublin," GoGo said. "Where do you think you're going?"

"Home."

"Come back here," Ivan said. "Do you think for one second that we're going to Le Bernardin without our girl?"

THE SPACE BETWEEN

ON SUNDAY MORNING, FIVE QUICK RAPS SMACKED AT PEPPA'S BEDROOM DOOR. She played dead. No doubt her mom wanted to remind her of what a spectacular human being the plumber was. He'd started out as your basic nice guy but as the week progressed, her mom tried to convince her that his IQ had miraculously increased to just short of Einstein. Footsteps receded and within a few minutes, the car doors slammed. What with a full Mass, her parents would be gone for a couple of hours. And it was rare that Peppa had the house to herself, so she rolled over in bed and listened to the squirrels messing about in the crawl space between the ceiling and the roof. She hadn't bothered to tell her dad about the nest because, just like the mold, very soon squirrels also wouldn't be her problem. She eyed Virginia's books stacked on her night table. Last night she'd stayed up past two and finished *Between the Acts*. And if she dispensed with the plumber as planned, she'd be starting Virginia's diaries within the hour. Peppa shoved her feet into slippers and scuffed to the bathroom thinking, *Dear Virginia, I'll be right back*.

Her parents had showered consecutively, so she opened a screenless window to dissipate the steam still trapped in the small bathroom. Dirt from the outside sill promptly flew in, and a speck lodged in her eye. She ran water at the sink to rinse it out, but the more she splashed the more irritated her eye became. Leaning toward the mirror for a closer look, Peppa noticed that the iris in the afflicted eye had drifted about a quarter inch toward her nose. Maybe circling in either direction would snap it back into place. But after several orbits, no such luck. Which caused Peppa to wonder, had she *always* been cross-eyed?

There are many terrible ways women will contort themselves into the creatures that society deems acceptable; yet we must. Indeed, we must.

Peppa tried not to think about her face, much less look at it again. But thanks to Virginia's prompt, she was reminded of what she meant to do, and the plumber called for extraordinary measures. At random, she plucked a dark grey eye shadow from her mom's ancient stockpile of cosmetics. After drawing thick circles around her eyes, she added wings at the outer edges. Might as well fill in her brows too. When she stepped back from the mirror to assess the overall impact, a vampire looked back at her. If the goth makeup didn't put him off, the crossed eyes surely would. Now the doorbell rang—Christ in a wheelchair, the guy was ten minutes early. Peppa ran to her bedroom and floated the blowsiest dress she owned over her body, skipped down the stairs, and waited for his fourth ring before opening the door.

The plumber towered over Peppa—had to be six foot. She'd imagined a shrimp. And his body, as much of it as she could see under a denim jacket and a pair of paint-speckled white pants, was trim. She'd imagined a fatty. He had a Roman nose, and his eyes bulged in a way that made her think of hypertension. Thin, almost nonexistent, lips. Brown hair, and a reddish beard gone to seed at least a few days. If he hadn't even bothered to shave, Peppa wondered if he was going through the motions too. She stood aside and waved him into the house. He walked straight through to the kitchen as if he'd been there before, and sat in her dad's chair. What balls. An iffy start, but this was a good thing.

"I think we have pastries somewhere. Tea or coffee?" she asked, not bothering with introductions.

"Tea would be grand."

Peppa filled the kettle and located the pastry bag her mom had labeled *Peppa's Date on Sunday.* She peeked inside. "Chocolate croissants."

"Bittersweet?" he asked.

Pushy bastard. "I'm not sure."

She cleared her parents' breakfast plates from the table and purposely let them clatter loudly into the sink. He flinched. She tore off squares of paper towels and let them float onto the table. One landed on the floor. The plumber rescued his "napkin" and placed it with some ceremony on his lap. Pretentious faker. While waiting for the water to boil and the croissants to warm in the toaster oven, Peppa sat across from him. She dragged the Sunday paper closer and began to read the lead article about a potential garbage strike.

"Well. I'm Brendon."

"I know," she said without looking up.

"I just arrived."

"So my mom said."

"You were born here, right?"

"Uh-huh."

"Your mom's quite a dear. I met her at my cousin's wedding."

Peppa shoved the paper away. "Melanie. A truly heinous person."

"I find her that too. Anyway, turns out your mom made me feel a little less homesick that day."

"You're missing Ireland?"

"God yeah," he said. "I'd go back tomorrow if I could."

"So, why don't you?"

"It's a bit complicated."

The toaster oven dinged. She piled the pastries into a basket at the middle of the table, then poured hot water into mugs. They dunked tea bags for so long that the motion became synchronized. Peppa was committed to staying the course with the dunking, so it was the plumber who finally broke rhythm. He tossed his teabag over his shoulder without looking, and it splatted as it landed in the sink. She didn't react and thought, how pathetic that he'd spent time practicing such a ridiculous trick.

"So, what do you do?" he mumbled while squishing an entire croissant into his mouth.

"I work at an investment firm. In Manhattan." It seemed important to add that detail.

He chewed and swallowed a few times, then cleared his throat. "Do you like it?"

"Sure."

"Mind if I have another croissant? I'm starving."

"Suit yourself." She nudged the basket half an inch closer to him.

"The situation. Where I'm living? It's—"

"*Complicated*?"

Now he laughed. "I was reaching for *strange*. But it's actually worse than that. My uncle's a drunk. His wife is a thief. Melanie's a fekkin' blight to the human race. And I've no toilet in the shithole I'm living in."

Aside from the toilet part, none of this was news to Peppa. The one and only time the Maloney clump came to dinner was ages ago, back when her mom was still having an occasional decent patch. She'd grossly miscalculated the baking time of a casserole, so they ended up eating after nine. Which provided ample opportunity for Maloney to get out-of-his-gourd drunk and stare nonstop at Peppa's chest, though there was nothing of consequence to see at the time. And for Melanie to set a world record for answering every single question with one word—*dunno*. And, for the wife to wander upstairs unsupervised. The next day, Peppa's mom noticed her pearl choker had gone missing. Now it seemed the Maloney tribe was a fully formed quartet—a sot, a moron, a cat burglar, and a plumber minus a toilet.

"Tell me about the thief," Peppa said.

"The wife? Jesus. Where do I start? Well, you know that my uncle cannot make a living, right?"

"Not specifically, but it makes sense."

"He's a piss-poor painter who can barely tell black from white. And twenty days of the month, he's sleeping off the booze till noon. Except when your dad hires him for a job he can't possibly screw up, but always does. Then your dad calls me in to do 'touch-up,' which is code for a complete do-over. So, they've got no real money coming in. But they've got me living like a feral beast above the garage, paying half the mortgage."

"But the *wife*," she prodded.

"Have you been in their house lately?"

"Only once. And I'd rather forget it entirely." In fact, it was a few days after that dinner. Her dad had asked her to deliver a check to Maloney. He pulled Peppa into the front vestibule and tried to convert the non-boob stare into a real-time non-boob grab. The guy must have been fantastically farsighted. But just as his hand got close, Peppa kicked his shin. Then she crumpled up the check and threw it toward the thief, who was in the kitchen, stirring something on the stove.

"My uncle made a pass at you?" the plumber guessed.

"*Yes*. How'd you know?"

"Because he's constantly telling me about all his supposed conquests. He'd brag about humpin' a tree branch if the wind blew it in his direction. It's all fiction, of course. Anyway, with the amount of booze in his veins, I'm sure his dick hasn't been horizontal since Virginia Woolf's last novel was published."

"What?" Peppa gasped.

"Sorry. Didn't mean to be so crude."

"No, it's not that. I just finished that book. *Between the Acts.*"

"Oh, Virginia's grand, isn't she? Anyway, the house. You wouldn't believe the stuff crammed in there. Utter nonsense. Miniature toiletries. Like toothpaste, lotion, shampoo, hand wipes, breath spray. Hundreds of D batteries. Even bras and jock-straps. Oh, and condoms. Piles and piles of junk taking up entire floor surfaces. And I couldn't figure out why they'd buy all this crap. Or even where they'd gotten the money. But here's the thing: I started noticing the wife leaving the house wearing bulky overcoats. No matter the weather, she bundles up like it's cold enough to snap her tits off. Peppa, she's a bloody effin' pickpocket!"

"No."

"I'm absolutely convinced."

"This is too good," Peppa said.

"Isn't it? And Melanie's involved on the resale end. About once a week, a beat-up SUV with blackened windows shows up. The driver never gets out. Melanie's hopping all over the place. Dragging garbage bag after garbage bag from the house. Tossing them into the back end of the car. The wife's lurking on the stoop like some kind of lookout. I can see it all from my window."

"That's pretty shocking, but in a way, not. I've always considered them pretty rough trade."

"Complete deadbeats. I don't have the heart to tell my family back in Ireland. They have a near-perfect notion of my uncle." He reached out his hand, then retract-ed it quickly. "Okay if I eat that last croissant?"

He'd already scarfed four to her one. "Go ahead. But if you want . . . I guess I could make us some eggs."

"God, that'd be super. I've not had a hot meal in ages."

"No kitchen up there?"

"Nope. I'm eating Dinty Moore out of a can. Tuna fish too. Mayo seems to last pretty well without a fridge."

"No *refrigerator*?"

"And no water. I have to go down to the garage slop sink. I'm pissin' on a dead tomato patch in the backyard just to avoid going in their house."

"It sounds illegal. Does my dad know?"

"No. And don't tell him."

"But how can Maloney make you live like this? Really, my dad should know."

"I want it kept simple with your dad. I'm a good plumber, and he saw it immediately. He's been a lifesaver, getting me on the jobs. Whatever he needs, even painting, I do it. So, please. Keep it between us?"

"Okay, I won't say anything."

She opened the refrigerator and set a carton of eggs on the counter.

"Listen, I don't mean to be forward," he said, "but do you happen to have any bacon? You know, to go with the eggs?"

She dug into the back and pulled out a package of Oscar Meyer. "Will this do?"

"You're an angel," he said, stifling a yawn. "And while you're cooking, mind if I have a quick lie-down on your sofa over there?" He pointed to the den adjacent to the kitchen. "I'm exhausted, and it's nice and warm in here."

"No heat?"

"It's almost impossible to sleep in a cold room."

He stretched out, and in less than a minute was in full snore mode. Peppa fried the bacon, reserving the fat to sauté mushrooms and red peppers that would fill the omelets. She toasted two kinds of bread—whole wheat and cinnamon raisin—then stacked the buttered slices in the now-empty croissant basket. Anticipating that coffee would be his next demand, she brewed some espresso Ivan swore was like taking an injection of adrenaline.

Just when she was about to fold over the second omelet, he woke up and headed toward the bathroom. The water ran for quite some time. He returned, dragging his fingers through damp hair.

"I feel much better, thanks."

She plated the meal and poured some orange juice. "How *do* you shower?"

"Oof. Busted," he said, cringing. "I did a sponge-off in your loo. Hope you don't mind—my pits had gone gamey. Maloney's got a family membership to the local Y. I shower there on the days I'm not working."

Breakfast was dealt with quickly and in silence. When they took their coffees into the den, he dropped into her dad's club chair and gave her a sheepish smile. And Peppa thought, *good*. He should be embarrassed, because not only had he been fed, but he'd also taken a power nap and pretty much bathed in her powder room. What else was he going to help himself to? Her dad's closet for a change of clothes? But since he really did seem to be having a hard time and there was no possibility she'd ever see him again, she decided to give him another half hour of her time. The problem was, other than the local degenerates, she couldn't imagine they had a thing in common to talk about.

It is a great shock that my books are now known; which soothes, and in the oddest of ways, shames; and I shan't bother reconciling the two.

Peppa thought, *Oh, right.*

"What did you think of that book?" she asked. "Virginia's, that is."

"Clever. The play within the novel. And the use of verse. Lovely." He took a gulp of espresso.

"I thought so too."

"And the sexual ambivalence between Giles and Isa is interesting." Another gulp.

"Um, I suppose so."

"And then her attraction with the farmer," he added.

"Okay . . . right."

"But all they do is stare at each other." Third gulp.

"Yeah, the staring—"

"Oh! Not that I know anything about ambivalence . . . I mean the husband-and-wife sort . . . or . . . staring." Final gulp.

"Whatever."

"It's just that . . . well, I'm absolutely mad over Woolf," he said, "and . . . I don't get to talk to anybody . . . I mean, about her books—"

"Will you please stop *jabbering*?"

"Okay . . . I'll try . . . but what's in this coffee?"

"It's espresso."

"It's making me really jumpy. Anyway, it all started with *Mrs. Dalloway.* On the recommendation of the librarian. At the library. The one with the grey hair. And the bun. Anyway. At first, I went there just to sit in a comfortable chair. In a warm room. One day she came over, and I thought she was gonna kick me out. See, my clothes are usually dirty. From work, that is. I could easily be mistaken for a bum. But she only asked if I wanted something to read. And we got to talking. That's how I got into her.

I mean, Virginia. Sorry. And there you have it. My God. This *coffee*."

"How old are you, anyway?" Peppa asked.

"Why? I mean, what does it matter?"

"It's just, you seem . . . youthful. And your face is hard to read."

"Twenty-four. You?"

"Twenty."

"I'd have thought much older."

Peppa's jaw dropped two inches.

"God, no. Not your *face*. No. What I mean is, you're very mature."

"How can you even tell?" she sniffed. "I've barely said a thing."

"Yeah, I guess I have been talking a lot. It's the coffee. It's like speed. Mind you, I tried that only once. And a long time ago. But I couldn't stop vacuuming the living room rug."

"Fascinating."

"Anyway, the way you pay attention. It's unusual."

"Curiosity is simply a sign of good manners."

"Wait. You think I'm impolite?"

Peppa shrugged. "Maybe."

"Well, I really *do* want to know about your job."

"Okay, what do you want to know?"

"Is it a ton of pressure?" he asked.

"I'd say it's intense."

"Does your boss have a big staff?"

"Just the two of us."

"So, it's what, investments?"

"I'm not at liberty to say."

"Criminy. You're not making this easy."

"Why do you need this to be *easy*?"

"C'mon, Peppa. What the hell gives?"

She *was* being a perfect brat. "Okay, I can tell you this much. We do philanthropic work. And it's very important. For certain populations, it's potentially life-changing."

"Wow. You're only twenty and it sounds like an honest-to-God future. I feel like

I'm going down a toilet. If Maloney would ever install one. I'd settle for a sink. At least I could piss in it."

"Well, for what it's worth," Peppa said, "my dad thinks you're good. He's impressed with your skills and work ethic. And plumbers can make a ton of money. I mean, it's an evergreen profession."

"Maybe. Things feel pretty iffy at the moment."

"Look. If I can do well, you can too."

"Why wouldn't you do well?"

"Okay. Stop."

"What do you mean?" he asked.

"*Look* at me."

"I'm looking."

"I'm not exactly Nicole Kidman."

"Who is? Besides Nicole Kidman?"

"Don't be a brute!"

"I don't get it. What'd I do?"

"Don't make me spell it out."

"You're gonna have to, because I've no idea what's just happened."

As is habit, I tend to interrogate those around me; about the verisimilitudes of life and so on. But really, I am the only source for the actual truth.

Oh Virginia, Peppa thought. *I will tell the truth, and I will use myself as the source. I will.*

"Well, to begin with," she said, "I can't reasonably blame you for your endless gaffes in manners, because we don't get to choose how we're raised, and maybe even who we become. And you should know that when we end this entire charade of a date in about three minutes, I'll easily forgive you. But for the benefit of all the women you'll try to date in the future, I'm going to fill you in on some important facts. We, that is, women, come in many gradations of thick and thin, and a wide spectrum of staggering beauty at one extreme and flat-out homely on the other. I won't demean either of us by pointing out the obvious benefits of super good looks paired with a smashing body. Having said that, all is not lost. For example, if you're overweight but gorgeous, things will work out. If you're regular-looking and thin enough, life will also go pretty well.

"But the way *I* look? My weird teeth and problematic eye? A plain Jane with a body the contour of a cylinder? My hair being the only thing worth admiring? Well, there are slim odds that I'll achieve what most consider a reasonable life, which includes a husband and kids. But here's the thing: I know I won't snare that husband, a fact I came to terms with a long time ago. And much to my parents' horror, I've never had any desire to pop out a string of whiners. All that being said, a miracle has happened. I landed a job I absolutely love. And no one has the power to mess that up. Certainly not the likes of *you*.

"So, let's be crystal clear. I know what this date is all about. My parents are desperate to get me hitched, and they don't particularly care to whom. Enter you, Mr. Plumber. And while I'll admit that you seem like a decent enough guy, I also know a fake and a fraud when I see one. Because I very much doubt that you live like Attila the Hun above Maloney's garage. And as much as I'd like to believe all this stuff about a mother-daughter scam, I happen to know that Melanie and her mom work shifts at the Dollar Store. And spare me your Good Samaritan librarian fairy tale, because there is no one working at that library who has grey hair. Much less a *bun*. And don't even imagine that I swallow this supposed-admiration-of-Virginia-Woolf BS. My mom is not above feeding you those storylines to trick me into thinking we actually have something in common. And just to pull the final trigger on this whole sorry shoot-out of a date, I'm dead certain that I know much more about toilets than you ever will!"

Peppa had covered her eyes with her hands at the beginning and held them there throughout. Now tears oozed between her fingers. Snot dripped from her nose. She cried and heaved until she could barely take another breath. When she finally did quiet down, she still couldn't open her eyes.

"Are you all right?" he asked.

His voice was so close she felt his breath on her face. She opened her eyes and found the plumber kneeling in front of her. She wiped the snot from her upper lip with her palm. He handed her a purple handkerchief similar to the one GoGo had blotted his forehead with when he was swooning over the Gramercy Tavern steak.

After blowing her nose, she asked, "Are you gay?"

Brendon laughed so hard he tipped backwards and landed against the club chair.

"I'm not. And you've got a ton of other ideas about me that also aren't true. What in God's creation brought all this on?"

Peppa wanted to make a joke of it and brush it all away. But he hadn't left. Also, there was Virginia's bit about truth-telling. "I'm afraid."

"Of me?"

"I don't know. Was I terribly cruel?"

"Don't you know what you said?"

"Not really," she said. "Some stuff about the way girls look? Wait, did I call you a brat?

"Worse. A brute."

"And there was something about pulling a trigger . . . God, did I threaten to *shoot* you?"

"Not exactly, but forget all that. Just tell me what you're afraid of."

"It's . . . um . . . *complicated*?"

He scrambled off the floor and sat facing her at the far end of the sofa. "See, this is why I think I like you. One second, you're spewing some bizarre manifesto on male-female attraction, the next you're bawling your eyes out. And then you're referencing a word I used an hour ago and it's already become an inside joke."

"If you want to leave, I'd understand. If we see each other on the street, we can wave. But can you at least forgive me?"

"I can and I will. And I'm not leaving."

Peppa pulled her legs up underneath herself and plucked her dress away from her belly. "That's very nice of you," she said primly.

"Listen, people sometimes say things they don't mean, especially when they're angry. And you sounded angry. But they're just words, Peppa. Not facts."

"Whatever words I said, I'm pretty sure I didn't mean them. Or most of them, anyway. But it's all my mom's fault. I've endured tons of these setups."

"Well, just so you know, this isn't a setup. I talked to your mom for a long while that day. And she mentioned you a lot. She said you've got a beautiful heart."

"No. My mom would never say that about me."

"I believe the exact phrase was that you had a *forgiving* heart. She was telling me that no matter what happens, you always forgive her."

"That's true enough."

"Anyway, it was *me* asking, not your mom. And there *is* a librarian with grey hair and a bun."

Peppa cocked her head, perplexed. "I haven't been to the library in years."

"Boy, you really don't remember. But are you still afraid? Or angry?"

"I don't know."

"Want to go for a walk on the beach? It must be warmer by now."

"Sure. Anyway, my parents will be home soon, and I don't want them to see us together."

"Damn, Peppa. If the only reason you'll go on a walk with me is because you don't want them to see us having a decent time, then forget it. I may be a dumb Irish lug, as some part of you believes, but you're not the only one with feelings."

Confusion reigns down on me daily, hourly, minute to minute; I dream my confusion. Perhaps the way towards sane thinking, if only as a temporary measure, is to consider that others are confused as well; or at the very least, benign.

Okay. Maybe there was a possibility that he had walked into the situation with a *perhaps something to gain, certainly nothing to lose* mindset. But she couldn't reasonably blame him for that, because *she'd* walked in cradling a bomb behind her back. And it was really sweet that he'd shown an interest in her mom, especially because most people avoided her as if her illness were contagious. And that he'd had the guts to ask for eggs and bacon, and a nap and a rinse? That was actually weirdly impressive. But mostly, if he could forgive her for all the stuff she'd spewed—whatever it was—then maybe she owed it to him to leave open the possibility that he wasn't the loser she'd assumed.

"I want to take the walk because . . . it might be fun," she said.

When they reached the beach, they removed their shoes and socks and stuck them into Peppa's knapsack. They skirted the edge of the surf, and she stumbled over an uneven mound of rocks at the cusp of the tide's reversal. He grabbed her by the elbow, then slid his hand down to hers and kept it there. She wasn't sure how first-date handholding typically went. The others had ended within the hour and certainly with no body contact. But before she could think of a reciprocal move, he threaded his fingers between hers and squeezed hard. Further down the beach, a strong breeze picked up against their backs. He gathered her hair up to keep it from flying into her face and stuffed it inside the collar of her coat. Then he draped his arm around her shoulder, and she allowed herself to sink closer to him. It was then that Peppa told him how ashamed she was of her earlier behavior. *All* of it, she emphasized. And he admitted to being afraid too. The *entire* time, he added.

The plumber lived in a decent-sized, but largely empty, room. A single bed lay against the longer wall, and a plastic folding table was opposite, sitting below two windows facing Maloney's house. Half the table was covered with canned goods and boxed food, plastic utensils, paper cups and plates. A folding chair had been tucked at the other end, where Peppa assumed the plumber ate his meals of Dinty Moore's gruel and Chicken of the Sea. In one corner, three suitcases lay on the floor with the tops open. His clothing had been nicely folded and separated. Pants in one, shirts in another. Underwear and other sundries in the third. Just two pairs of shoes; paint splatter covered one, and the other looked to be standard-issue construction boots. Then Peppa remembered the worst of what he claimed about the way he lived, and quickly glanced around to confirm that there was no plumbing of any sort. Yet, the walls were pale green, the trim a bright white—a cheerful combination that somehow worked to counteract the transient feel of the place.

Because the room was chilly and somewhat damp, Peppa followed his lead and kept her coat on. He gestured for her to sit on the bed, then dragged the chair over for himself. She saw the library books lying on the floor—*Between the Acts* and *Mrs. Dalloway*. Also, a hairbrush, a nail clipper, and a wastebasket stuffed to overflowing with crumpled tissues. Now this felt much too real, and Peppa lost some of her ease; she was sitting on a guy's bed, where he yawned and slept and woke and stretched. Probably scratched his balls, maybe picked his nose too, and whatever else he did to release bodily urges she didn't want to think about. She had never allowed herself to even imagine an intimate situation with a guy. And then she wondered, was it allowed for an unattractive girl like her to change her mind and walk out?

"If you want, I can fetch us some water from the garage sink," he offered. "I would have been more prepared, but I didn't know we'd end up here."

"No thanks. Nothing." She shivered and pulled her coat tighter.

"It's probably colder in here than out there," he said, pointing to the window. "Shifts in temperature like today never seem to make it inside. I can't wait for spring. I've been told it's the nicest season in New York."

Suddenly, the clichéd topic annoyed her. So much so that she remembered Liz Taylor as Martha and the plan to ditch him. "Yeah, we get all sorts of weather patterns and different temperatures and four whole seasons here on the East Coast. God bless America." She twirled her finger.

"Why the sarcasm?"

"The weather? Really?"

"Oh. Right." He looked embarrassed, then recovered immediately. "But it actually does affect me."

"Yes, I know. I'm sitting here. With my coat on. Shivering to pieces. Still, that doesn't make it interesting."

He sighed as if to say *here we go again.* "What's wrong now?"

"Not a thing."

"Is this what I'm in for? A smart-assed girl with a chip on her shoulder?"

She shrugged. "Maybe."

"Why are you throwing crap in my face? All I want is someone to talk to. Maybe be a friend."

"But you squeezed my hand. You put your arm across my shoulder. You even touched my *hair.*"

"Well, yeah, I did."

"That should mean something."

"It does. It means I like you," he said.

"You like me. Right. Same as you like my mom? Or the librarian? Did you hold their hands? Did you touch their hair? Did you go for walks on the beach with them? Did you invite *them* to this freezing-cold room too?"

"Wow. Are you gonna be like this forever?"

"Probably."

Suddenly he crossed his legs and arms simultaneously—whether a defensive posture or to give her what-for, Peppa couldn't tell which.

"You know what?" he said. "I'd like to talk to one of your former boyfriends."

"What? You stop it right there—"

"Because I need some advice."

"Cut it out."

"Yeah. See, first, I'd like to know at what stage of the game you'll get tired of shovin' shite down my throat. And second, at what point it'll be safe enough for me to love you."

"Why are you even *saying* that?"

"Saying what?" He cocked his head, all innocence.

"About boyfriends. And love."

"I'm saying whatever the hell I please. And how does *that* feel?"

"Really cruel."

"Swallow a dose of your own poison, Peppa. And by the way—I am not by nature a cruel person. I'm not so sure about you."

Peppa squinted at him. She tried not to cry. Then, like a miracle, he smiled—his eyes kinder than she deserved.

One's delusions, one's self-deception, one's inability to see, truly see, are fodder for a misery of one's own making.

"I'm terrified," she whispered.

"I get that."

"I've never had a boyfriend."

"Doesn't surprise me."

"Please be nice."

"Give me a reason," he said.

"Because I like you too."

"Convince me."

Peppa dropped her head. What did that mean? She took a stab. "Sit on the bed with me?"

When he didn't move, she patted the space beside her in that kind of beckoning signal she'd seen in rom-coms, except it was usually the guy—somebody like George Clooney—doing the patting. Now he joined her and pulled the pillows from beneath the covers, placing them behind their backs. And when she offered her hand, he accepted it without hesitation. Now sitting side by side, they stared out the window, watching clouds drift behind Maloney's roof, and Peppa was grateful for the respite from a drama she knew was of her own making. In time, the plumber turned toward her and placed his palm on her cheek. This was a move she couldn't recall seeing in any movie, so she decided to interpret it as unique and hoped that the plumber was sincere.

And now she thought back to what he had confessed on the beach. How his sister had been diagnosed with cancer a second time and how he had been sent here specifically to make enough money to pay for the costly experimental drug they all hoped would save her life. At the time, she'd wondered if he was telling the truth. But now she saw what a cynical notion that was. And so unfair. Because of *course* his sister was deathly ill, and maybe he *wasn't* a loser like his cousin, the heinous Melanie. And oh, if she could loosen the majority of her fears, this might just be the moment that she'd do the bravest thing ever, ever, ever. Then, as if he'd read her mind, his lips covered hers.

The kissing was both thrilling and endless. With her eyes slammed shut, Peppa heard nothing but their erratic breathing. She felt only the insistent pressure of his face against hers. She tasted a background of bacon. And there seemed to be an unspoken agreement between them that their saliva should mingle, that their teeth should click, and that their tongues were probes for exploration. And that the kissing was meant to keep all of these wondrous sensations going. Then thirty minutes in, or maybe it was only five, she pulled away for a breather and to have a peek. To her shock and relief, the plumber was grinning—a goofball expression, as in *look Mom, no hands*. That's when the laughter started, everything from giggle to guffaw. And soon enough, Peppa's belly muscles ached so deeply that her body became limp. She tipped over. The plumber collapsed with her, landing behind. He reached around and gathered her body close to his. As he breathed into the back of her head, she could still smell the bacon. And she could feel his erection. He pressed his groin against her just once, then abruptly disengaged and sat up.

"Let's have a rest," he said softly.

"Oh yes, I'm so glad you said that." She rolled onto her back and stretched her legs across his lap, which for some reason made him laugh again. "Don't start up," she pleaded. "I can't take any more."

"No, I was just thinking how funny that it's a lot warmer in here now. But don't worry. I won't say another word about the weather, your least favorite topic." He started to hum a low-pitched tune, and within seconds ramped up to a squeaky falsetto.

"Is that 'Singin' in the Rain'?" she asked. "I love that movie."

"I'm amazed you recognize it. My entire family's tone-deaf. Well, except for my sister. She had a fine ear." He paused and shook his head. "Listen to me. I've put her in the past tense already."

"It was a slip. *Had* could easily have been *has*."

"God, I hate all of this—I mean how I live," he said.

"It *is* quite sad. But you're making the most of it."

"My family doesn't know about all this." He pointed around the room. "I tell them I'm living well. But every morning, my entire body aches to go back. I'm checking the fares for good deals at least twice a week. And I've come close. But they're counting on me. The thing is, I don't know if I'll be able to make enough money, and soon enough."

"Brendon. I'm so sorry."

He shot her a pained expression. "You've never said my name before now."

"I think you're right."

"Listen. Peppa. I really need to ask you something."

"Oh God."

"Nothing terrible. It's about your rant."

"My . . . rant?"

"When you told me off for three minutes straight."

"Oh, that. I was just letting off steam. Don't pay any attention."

"Purely as a feat of breath control, how could I not?"

She sighed. "What do you want to know?"

"Why do you think your face is *plain* and that your body is like a . . . *cylinder*?"

She dragged her legs off him and tucked herself into a ball. "I can't talk about that."

"Why not?"

"Please," she whispered.

"But I want to understand."

"My face. My body. They're not appropriate topics. Anyway, we just met."

"But it's not the first time I've seen you," he said.

"What do you mean?"

"I've seen you leave your house in the morning. It's so damned cold in here I can't sleep past five, so I do a power walk first thing. That local cabbie picks you up. Kevin's his name, I think."

"You're *watching* me?"

"Dear God. No. It's not like that at all."

"Men are always looking at me," she said with disgust.

"I can't say I blame them."

"Okay, this is beginning to get creepy." She tried to get off the bed, but he pulled her back.

"You're getting the wrong idea," he said. "I saw you only a few times. But I was curious. You barrel out of the house like you're headed for a five-alarm. And you look so pulled together."

"Now that's just pure nonsense."

"And I'm thinking, where is this good-looking woman running off to?"

"Okay, stop. You don't have to puff me up. I know what I am."

The plumber jumped off the bed, dug through one of his suitcases, and returned with a hand mirror. "I'm going to break this down for you."

"Break what down?"

"I'm gonna tell you what *I* see."

"No. I can't," she said.

"Of course you can."

He reshuffled them on the bed and positioned his head in such a way that they could both see her reflection in the mirror.

"First," he said, "your eyebrows are perfectly arched. I bet you don't even need to pluck them."

"That's true. Not that I'd ever bother."

"Okay, your eyes. If we looked up classic eye shapes in the *Encyclopedia Britannica*, they'd be a perfect example of almond."

"I'm sure there's no such entry in the *Britannica*."

"The *World Book*, then."

"Doesn't exist anymore."

"My parents have it in their living room."

"That's the Irish for you," she teased. "Always decades behind the States."

"Have you even been to Ireland?"

"No."

"Well, Miss Know-it-all, we have stuff like electricity and plumbing. And Keats and Joyce."

Peppa sighed. "Get on with it."

"Ever notice how high your forehead is?"

"Not once."

"And that you have an impressive widow's peak at your hairline?"

"The line of my hair is not interesting."

"The combination is quite fetching." He smiled as if a major victory had been achieved.

"So far, I'm finding this a thoroughly unremarkable exercise. And unconvincing because you've brushed right over the fact that I'm cross-eyed."

"I was getting to that. Lemme take a look." He set the mirror down and peered into her face, his gaze flitting from one eye to the other. "Just as I suspected. An optical illusion."

"Huh?"

"That eye is bloodshot toward the nose, which gives the illusion of the iris being off center. You're fine."

"I'm a freak."

"You're a nut!"

"Can we talk about the weather now?"

He laughed. "Nope. Your nose."

She sniffed. "What about it?"

He ticked off the main points with his fingers. "Fairly broad at the bridge. A slight upswing at the tip. Nostrils symmetrical. A couple of freckles. Purely Irish."

"Whatever you say," she said, yawning.

"I say."

"Okay, then! Guess that wraps it up." She pointed to the window. "And look. The weather. Clouds!"

"Yeah, cumulonimbus."

"How would you know *that*?"

"In addition to studying twentieth-century Irish history, which included the division of my beloved country, the IRA, the Troubles, the flip-flopper Gerry Adams and that murderer Margaret Thatcher, I also took an elective on atmospheric shifts and weather trends and climate change. *And clouds.* Got all that?"

Before Peppa could react, he positioned the mirror again and dragged his finger from her nose down to her upper lip. "And look at that. Your philtrum."

"My what?"

"The space between your nose and lip. Quite perky. And now it's drawing my attention to your lower lip. And that pout. And *that* makes me wanna do this." With his fingers, he gathered clumps of her hair like the reins on a horse, and pulled her to him.

"Careful!" she said, pushing him away. "Hair is my only decent feature."

"Rubbish." He lay down and patted the space beside him just as she had. Peppa smiled and joined him.

"You forgot about my front teeth," she said. "Try and spin that."

"I adore the left tooth. Rather fond of the right. But I have to confess that the aspect I'm mad about is the space between." He slid his hand up from the hem of her dress and settled it on her waist for a few seconds. His fingers hopped between her hip bones, then backed out. That took all of ten seconds. And now that the test drive seemed to be over, he retreated to the spoon position, behind her.

"Peppa."

"What."

"Why the hell are you wearing a dress three sizes too big?"

"I'm not."

"It's an upside-down sack with no relation to your body."

"I've gained weight since my job."

"I feel no fat whatsoever," he said.

"The dress fits."

"How can you say that?"

"Because it's true."

"Oh, God."

"Look at me."

When she turned around, the plumber cupped his hand at her ear and whispered, "You have a gorgeous face and a killer body. And, a quirky and maddening and completely wonderful personality. Peppa, you are a beautiful person. And all I want is for you to understand this."

Clothes flew around the room. They scrambled to get under the covers, and their bodies tangled into knots. He hugged her hard and wouldn't let go, long enough for Peppa to give in to the power of his lasso arms and fierce legs. They reprieved the kissing marathon for a time, then his mouth went everywhere else. And as she let it all happen, she kept her eyes closed so as not to see any regret that might flash across his face. Eventually he guided her hand to his penis, which was less scary than she'd feared because it wasn't completely hard. That was the moment she decided to trust the plumber, and she allowed him to push into her when he was able. She wanted it to be pleasurable but didn't mind that it hurt, because the words he'd said had eclipsed any physical discomfort. Words she never imagined she'd ever hear. And words she might, in the future, consider as some possible assemblage of the truth. But for now, Peppa was in the plumber's room, lying on his bed, and he was inside her. It was a place and a feeling a girl like her was lucky to experience.

And she thought, *Dear Virginia, could this be real?*

HOW WILL I KNOW?

THROUGHOUT THE PRECEDING MONTHS, STRAIGHT FLUSH HAD RUN, AND conquered, many gauntlets proposed by Peppa. And as they all approached the finish line, she found herself testing them in increasingly tricky ways. It wasn't as if she wanted them to fail. In fact she rooted for them. But Peppa was convinced that the best way to ensure their success was to make the vetting process not only difficult but also excruciatingly tiresome. As an example, just when she knew they assumed the project was close to being green-lit, she would send an email with *Just a few more questions!* in the subject line. And that email was typically no less than three pages, with maybe half a dozen attachments. She could practically hear the groans from across the country. Then the Toilets, as she and Ivan called them, would go silent for a few weeks, during which time Peppa then worried that her methods were excessive, even unfair. But they never complained and always came back with the right solutions. The Toilets had moxie.

Peppa and Ivan sat next to each other at a huge table in the biggest and fanciest conference room LBS offered. Eight thick binders, representing the sum total of the Toilets' work, had been spread across the length of the table. She closed her eyes. "I'm ready. Say the first title and then wait ten seconds before going to the next."

One by one Ivan called them out. Proposal. Concept. Data and Research. Functional Theory. Modifications. Production Specification. Final Costs. Final Scheduling. Though ten seconds was in no way time enough to visualize all the pages specifically, Peppa felt a deep sensation of familiarity. And if the situation did arise where Ivan asked her to quickly pluck a detail out of the air, she was confident that it would appear in her mind's eye.

"Peppa? Want to do it again?"

"No, but take Data and Research out altogether. I'm pretty sure we won't need it, and I don't want it in my sight line."

Ivan pulled the binder off the table then realigned the others. "The seeing part. I still can't wrap my head around that."

"It feels like an old habit. Like, something you can do with great precision but can't remember a thing about how or when you learned it."

"So you can't even remember when it started."

"No," she said. "Except I do have a memory of watching the pages turn while my dad read to me. All the words put together made a shape—either a rectangle or a square. Maybe that was the source. Anyway, geometry organizes lots of stuff in my head. The year and the months and the weeks, even the hours of the day are always circles. But triangles are my favorite. They're so efficient. No excess—pared to the bone. And the equilateral is just brilliant."

"I'd go nuts."

"No you wouldn't. But I don't consider it an advantage. It's never helped me in any way that mattered. Until now, I guess."

"Well, you've certainly figured the Toilets backwards and forwards. I've never been as confident about any project since I began the philanthropy."

"But Ivan, you do understand why I had to be super rigorous with them? That mistake at the beginning."

"Yeah, of course."

"They needed to get serious, and fast. And it was good for me too because I realized I had to be a few steps ahead of them."

"They must feel pretty beat up by now," he said.

"Hey! Don't go soft on me. Remember that email you sent on my first day?"

"Sure."

"It scared the crap out of me."

"I certainly didn't mean to do *that*."

"I know," she said. "But you took me seriously and so the stakes were very high. And that was intimidating. I wanted the Toilets to feel that kind of fear too, and right from the beginning."

"Have I created a sadist?"

"I hope not. But today I get to relax while *you* play bad cop. And I can't wait for dinner tonight. Where're we going, anyway?"

Ivan pulled on his shirt cuffs. He coughed and sniffed. He took a huge breath, released it slowly, and then finally, folded his hands like he was in church. "A guest is joining us."

"Oh?"

"GoGo."

"Oh. Fun! How is he?"

"Doing quite nicely, actually," he said. "But . . . well . . . you're going to think I'm ridiculous."

"Because?"

"I don't know how to say this . . ."

"Oh please. Out with it."

"GoGo is living with me."

"He is? Amazing!" Peppa squealed.

"He never left after that night. I know, I know. It's fast."

"I think it's fantastic."

"You knew?"

"I'm from Queens, not Siberia. I noticed you barely mentioned him after we went to Le Bernardin, so I figured something was up. Could have been good or bad. So I didn't ask."

"I'm still in a bit of shock," he said. "It's been exciting and sometimes awkward. But mostly really, really easy. Anyway, I made a reservation at Café Boulud. Neither of us have ever been, and we're dying to try it out. It'll be a double celebration. For you and the Toilets, and GoGo and me."

Just then, the doors opened and three teenagers walked in pushing a cart stacked with cardboard boxes. Peppa had never seen the Toilets before, not even in pictures; up till now they'd been only distinct voices behind emails. They appeared gaunt, almost malnourished, and weirdly, had stuck name tags on the front of their shirts. *Finn* still had peach fuzz for sideburns. *Zack* looked like he was getting over an acne outbreak. *Trevor* wore a cap with Bugs Bunny above the rim.

"Welcome!" Ivan said, gesturing for them to sit opposite him and Peppa. "Have a seat. And thanks for the name tags."

"People seem to mix us up," Finn explained.

"I'm sure it'll be helpful," Ivan said. "But just out of curiosity, and forgive me, how old are you all?"

"It's okay. People seem to think we're around sixteen. But we're twenty-one. We didn't go to college. We took a lot of gap years. We still live with our parents."

"At least you're legal," Ivan said, trying to suppress a smile.

"We get carded everywhere. It's a drag," Finn said.

"I imagine it is. How was the flight over?"

"We thought it seemed very long. We've never been to the East Coast. We can't believe we're here. We're very nervous. People back home seem to think we'll fail."

"Well, Peppa and I *seem* to think your project is really great," Ivan said. "You've done a ton of work, and we know it hasn't been easy. But unless something goes very wrong, you can relax, because for all intents and purposes this meeting is a formality. That said, today we're going to go over every detail. Peppa? Start the meeting, please."

What in the flockity hell? This was not what was supposed to happen. For the last several days, Ivan had made her explain everything to him. All so that *he* could run the meeting. He'd even said it out loud—*I. Will. Be. Running. The. Meeting.*

What can one say about men; other than they astound with their trickery.

"I don't understand this. What's going on?" Peppa said quietly.

Ivan swiveled his chair to face away from the Toilets. Peppa did the same. They put their heads together. "You're the one with a complete grasp of the project," he whispered. "I didn't want you to be nervous days before. I know what I'm doing, Peppa. Trust me." They swiveled back.

"Peppa's in charge," he announced. "Pay close attention to her."

When one is left feeling scuttled about in the most precarious way; in the end one must trust; perhaps even smile.

Peppa did trust Ivan. That part was easy. *But sorry, Virginia, in this case the smiling part is not going to happen.*

For the next couple of hours, she grilled them hard. In fact, she was close to ruthless. But the Toilets tolerated it with good nature and recited data like parrots and with complete comprehension. Plus, they were funny and dopey and innocent. All the while, Ivan said nothing and kept very still—kind of like a role reversal for their morning clients. When it was all over, everyone was in a festive mood, and the conversation turned personal. Trevor was a Seattle Seahawks fan. Zack was addicted to the HBO series *Six Feet Under*. And Finn expressed concern that he'd never grow a full beard. Ivan assured him that shaving was actually an annoyance. The other boys nodded in agreement, though Peppa suspected they'd agree to just about anything Ivan said. If she were on the brink of an enormous cash infusion, she'd nod like a bobble-head too. Finally, when it seemed there was nothing more to say, the Toilets stood up and began to put their laptops away.

"Hey guys, just one more question," Peppa said. "I'm curious about something. Did any of you consider the effect of elevation and climate on certain components of the toilet? Specifically, connectors and flanges."

The Toilets immediately plunked back down in their seats.

"I was thinking about it last week," she continued. "The working prototype you've based the whole shebang on was fabricated in Florida. That environment is humid and at sea level. The Navajo Nation is anywhere between four thousand to ten thousand feet above sea level and has no more than 20 percent humidity most of the year. So, I did some research. It turns out that the rubber and silicone materials you've specified have failed with other products because of that precise problem. And those failures occurred in much more favorable conditions than the Navajo Nation. Anyway, I found a company in Pittsburgh that's come up with a material that's able to withstand the outermost thresholds of elevation and moisture. Actually, they contributed to solving the faulty O-ring seal that caused the *Challenger* to blow up in 1986. It's a detail, but kind of important . . . Don't you think?"

Peppa noticed that Ivan was now standing across the room with his back against the wall as if to gain some distance from which to witness this potentially disastrous deal-breaker. While Trevor picked at a hangnail and Zack looked like he was going to cry, Finn began digging around in his backpack.

"Hang on," Finn said.

"I'm hanging on," Peppa said.

He pulled out a crumpled piece of paper and placed it on the table in front of her. Scribbled with a black Sharpie was the name of the company in Pittsburgh and the same contact Peppa had spoken with.

"Good. You caught it," she said.

Finn nodded, but he didn't look happy.

"Then why didn't you bring this up while we were discussing everything?" she asked.

"I'm the materials guy, and I was embarrassed that I'd caught it at the last minute. Like two days ago. I didn't say anything because I didn't want you to think badly of us. I mean, me. Trevor and Zack didn't know. I was hoping you wouldn't catch it. But you did. We think you're a genius, Peppa."

"I'm not a genius. I've just got the kind of brain that works well for this type of scrutiny."

"But what's going to happen now? Did I mess it up? I mean, do we lose the funding?"

Peppa looked at Ivan. His face remained inscrutable, and she figured it was still her meeting. "Progress is made mostly through making lots and lots of mistakes. And technically, it wasn't even a mistake, because you did catch it. So, this project is a go."

Trevor made a fist-pump, and Zack let loose a *yippee*. Finn put his hands over his face and sobbed so hard and for so long that Peppa felt compelled to give him a hug.

Once the Toilets left, they returned to Ivan's office to wait for GoGo. Ivan was uncharacteristically quiet, and she wondered if he might be nervous about presenting themselves as a couple.

"That was some chess match you just played," Ivan said.

"Oh. Was I wrong to do it that way?"

"No. It was a move that only someone with years of experience and tremendous confidence would have made. The way you held back, giving them room. Then when you saw they didn't have it, you simply explained the problem in a calm and reasonable way. *And*, and this is the key thing, Peppa, there was no disappointment or anger or frustration in your voice. No sense of a scolding or reprimand. The reason that's so important is because they walked away feeling that nothing had really gone wrong. You allowed them to maintain their dignity. And that's important as we move forward with them. So they can feel on equal ground. Not many people have the skills to do that, much less understand why such a skill is so valuable. Peppa, you're light years ahead. And something tells me you have no idea of your brilliance."

"I felt sorry for them, that's all. And I don't like for people to be sad. Don't make a thing of it. Please?"

"Sure, we can drop it. But one day I hope you'll stop dismissing who you are."

Now a man appeared at the door. It was GoGo, but at the same time, not GoGo. His eyebrows weren't a primary color, but basic brown. He wore a dark blue suit with a classic striped tie. A pair of sky-blue sneakers was the sole standout accessory. Standing on any NYC street, this GoGo would blend in with a lamppost.

"Hi there, GoGo," Peppa said.

"Yes, dear girl. 'Tis I. And you look glum."

"No, I'm fine. We just had a long meeting and I'm kind of wrung out."

"Did you tell her about us?" GoGo asked Ivan.

"Of course I did. Right before the meeting."

"What did she say?"

"She's pleased for us."

"Actually, I'm thrilled," Peppa corrected. "And GoGo, you've lost weight."

"Not a single pound," he countered. "A well-tailored suit will perform all manner of miracles. I'm finished with squeezing myself into Lagerfeld jumpsuits."

"Listen, I'm very hungry," Ivan said. "Let's catch up at Boulud."

"I hear that everyone's raving about the *blanquette de veau*," GoGo said.

How weird, Peppa thought. The old GoGo would never rely on *everyone's* opinion about anything, especially food.

"But what do they say about the service?" Ivan asked.

"How bad can it be?" GoGo said.

Wait. The old GoGo had zero bandwidth for anything but exceptional service.

"Should I call now to make sure we get a quiet table?" Ivan asked.

"Eh, what will be will be."

Huh? Just the idea of a noisy room was the old GoGo's version of Hell.

"Did you manage to get the laundry finished?" Ivan asked.

"Vacuumed too, and I polished—"

"Hold the Pledge," Peppa said. "What's with this men-on-happy-pills banter?"

Ivan looked nonplussed. "Um, we get along?"

"But you sound like you've just completed charm school for . . . newlyweds."

"Oh, Peppa," GoGo sighed. "Must you make an issue? Though I suppose it *is* difficult to explain."

"In a way that makes any kind of sense," Ivan added.

"Because how could we have known—"

"That we'd have this connection—"

"This ease—"

"This—"

"Now you're completing each other's sentences. Who *talks* like that?" Peppa said.

"Peppa, darling," GoGo said. "It's simple. Ivan and I are in love."

Oh, God. Since their date, she and Brendon had talked on the phone twice with this same startling degree of compatibility. They liked the same food and hated the same music. Neither were religious, but both believed in some kind of higher source. Peppa wanted to see the world, and Brendon wanted to make enough money to travel first class. Brendon had grown up landlocked and was afraid of the ocean, so Peppa promised to teach him how to swim. It was all cheerful, even hopeful. And, they finished each other's sentences. *That* was love?

"I had sex with Brendon," she said.

"Who in the Queen's name is *Brendon*?" GoGo asked.

"He's a plumber," Ivan said.

"A plumber? Gawd. "

"She went on a date with him to appease her parents. They have messed-up views about her future. And they don't like that she's working with me at all. It's been difficult."

"Well, aside from all that, and aside from this plumber, having sex on a first date could be a *whatever* or a *Holy Bejesus,* " GoGo said.

"Peppa, which is it?" Ivan asked. "I mean, how do you feel about him?"

"I'm not sure. But . . . how will I know?"

"Know what?"

"If I'm in love."

"Ooooh boy," GoGo said. "Ivan, you'd better eat a bag of nuts, because we're not leaving this office until this is properly dealt with. Out with it, dear girl."

"He was mostly amazing. I was a complete asshole."

"Generally, people don't want to have sex with assholes, Peppa," Ivan said.

"I improved."

"Details?"

"Well, we started at my house. I was grouchy. We walked on the beach, and that was okay. Then we ended up at his place. I put him through round two. And three and four. And even after all that, he was still so nice."

"So you managed to more or less get on the other side of conflicts. And then had sex," Ivan said.

"But I'm a virgin. I mean I *was* a virgin. And I've never even had a boyfriend. So I don't know the first thing about how it's supposed to go, let alone about love. But that word. Love. I can't get it out of my head. It never stops. Even when we were with the Toilets, Ivan. All I could think about was how it might be possible that I love Brendon. So I need you guys to explain it to me. I mean, what the hell is it?"

"Peppa, everyone experiences love differently. And it takes time to evolve," Ivan said.

"But it's only been two weeks and look at you both. It's obvious you love each other."

"Okay, in our case it *was* fast. But I'm not good at verbalizing this stuff. GoGo?"

"I'm not exactly a poster boy either. But the first thing that comes to mind is how comfortable I feel. I can relax. I don't have to be anything. And I remember how outrageous I was on stage and how adored I was for it. You do that for a couple of years and it'll bleed into your personal life in no time. But once Ivan and I got together, I realized how exhausted I was from propping up that . . . *person*. Maybe the plumber saw behind your façade. And maybe that's what you responded to—that he saw you."

"There were times when I felt that way," she said. "Kind of floaty. Like I didn't need to fix anything. But then I'd pick a fight and ruin it."

"But remember how horrid I was to GoGo when we were trying to get him out of my apartment? When I saw we had food in common, the barriers just dropped. Peppa, it's like a seesaw. You try to find that common balancing point and stay steady. And Brendon must be smart, otherwise you wouldn't consider him for a second."

"He is," she said. "I think he might be smarter than me."

"What's he look like?" Ivan asked.

"Nice. But also, kind of . . . odd."

"Looks are overrated," GoGo said.

"Desire begins between the ears," Ivan added.

"Don't criticize in the sack," GoGo said.

"Right. Discuss it later," Ivan said.

"Whoa! This is way too much. And where are you getting this stuff?" she asked.

"Dr. Ruth," they said in unison.

"You guys are so cute," Peppa said. "But GoGo, will I ever hear another hyperbolic rant of indignation out of your mouth again?"

"I guess I have eased up. Or better to say, I have—forgive the self-help jargon—recovered my authentic self. But given the correct provocation, I assure you that I'll act upon my right as a washed-up rock star holding residency in no less than three countries, to opine, perhaps even unleash, on certain matters of egregious effrontery."

"See, Peppa?" Ivan said. "He's still there. Just a bit reshuffled."

THE BLIND GAME

THEY'D MADE A PLAN TO MEET AT BRENDON'S PLACE MIDAFTERNOON, AND Peppa found herself walking the beach about an hour before she was due to arrive. She didn't know why. Maybe because she had to get out of the house, what with her mom and dad going on and on every half-hour about how elated they were that she agreed to a second date. As if their sole purpose for living had finally landed from Heaven above, directly onto her shoulders. Or, simply to bask in the unseasonably warm weather, which felt like a gift. But really, it was none of that. After the mini tutorial / pep talk from Ivan and GoGo, Peppa still didn't know if the way she felt about Brendon was love. And walking on the beach reminded her of some movie where a girl was trying to decide something about a boy and somehow, a beach conveniently appeared. That girl took the walk, and then she knew. In most movies, it worked out that way.

Peppa scanned the sky. Not a cloud to be named, and the sun beat down with as much heat as its current distance from the earth allowed. She'd not worn a coat and barely needed the wool sweater she'd tied around her waist. During their most recent phone call, Brendon had promised to buy another blanket. But she expected that he wouldn't remember, which is why she brought the sweater.

In Sandy Point, the wind typically kicked up after the noon hour. Some fathers were taking advantage, stringing up kites. The kids were ecstatic. But those playing a game of badminton were thwarted by unpredictable downdrafts. Nobody made points. Suddenly, damp air at least ten degrees cooler barreled off the water. Clouds gathered quickly, and the jig was up for everyone. Peppa dug her arms into the sweater. She tilted her face to the sun and, with her eyes closed, began walking. It was a game she played when she was very young, when her mom assured her that the beach was so wide she'd never get lost. She'd never be hurt. That's what her mom said. And now Peppa remembered that Christmas Day again, when, after the seashell game, they'd played the blind game for the very last time.

Oh, how many times do I look and look and never see; until the time when I do see and then dearly wish I hadn't.

Peppa opened her eyes. There it was—the bench. Repainted many times over the years, currently red. She sat down. It wasn't often that she thought about the bench; in fact, she tried hard to avoid the memory. But when it did break through, it presented itself like a movie short with a black-and-white vérité feel. In this way she could remain an observer, the whole episode viewed as if from the back row of a theater. And so there were doubts. Was this really the bench? There were others not so far away, after all. How was it possible to fill up a bucket with seashells? Perusing the sand now, she saw very few. Had her hands and feet actually been near to complete frostbite? She flexed her fingers as if to prove they were fine, perhaps always had been. And did her mom really tell her to close her eyes and make believe she was blind? Sometimes Peppa even wondered if the memories had been implanted by her dad when he eventually told her what had happened, and the truth about her mom and her illness. But as Peppa shivered from the strong breeze penetrating the loose weave of her sweater, she did remember this damp and cold wind. And also the voice who, for the very first time, gave her three simple directives: **Hold on. Keep breathing. Stay alive.** Peppa had always held tightly to these six words that she knew had saved her life. And also to the distinctive voice who eventually identified herself as Virginia.

Her phone rang. "I'm so sorry, Brendon," she said as she picked up the call.

"Where are you?" he asked.

"On the beach, and I walked too far in the opposite direction. I'll be there in fifteen minutes. No. Make that ten. I'll run."

"Don't run. I got back from the grocery store just a few minutes ago myself, so I'm still setting stuff up."

"What stuff?"

"Food. Drinks. I got that blanket. And another folding chair so we don't have to eat sitting on the bed. Also . . . Peppa Ryan?"

"Yes?"

"*Hurry.*"

She ran as fast as she could, almost falling twice, making it in under ten minutes. Approaching the backyard by the side of the house, she ducked below the windows so the Maloney freaks wouldn't see her. When Brendon opened the door, she fell onto the bed, panting like a hound.

"You nut. I told you not to run," he said, laughing.

"Last word out of your mouth was *hurry*."

"I hope you're hungry."

"Just a little. Oh, are *you*?"

"I'm famished. But Peppa, first I need to say something to you. And it's really important. Ready?"

"Uhhhh . . . depends on what it is."

"*Ca bhfuil an leithreas.*"

"Huh?"

"It means, where is the toilet. In Gaelic."

"How . . . useful."

"You're Irish. You should at least know some stock phrases for when you visit. My parents will love it." He pulled a piece of paper from his backpack. "And look. Here's a list. Stuff we can do today. I've been carrying it around for days. Adding things."

Peppa perused. "I don't think we can do all this in one day."

"We'll do as much as we want. But can we eat first? I really am starving. There's soda in the refrigerator. Pull it out while I get the sandwiches together."

"A fridge?" Peppa looked around. At the other end of the room stood a chest of drawers and an upholstered chair, along with the refrigerator. "Hey, did you rob a bank?"

"Oh, yeah, the furniture."

"The place looks almost normal. Where'd you get the money?"

"Your dad put me on a huge job. There's five bathrooms. He needed a crew of plumbers."

"I know that job. I priced it out. The client's bonkers."

"I wouldn't know about that," he said, "but a couple weeks of solid work was enough to buy a few things. And yeah, I own a half fridge now. Best invention ever. After the toilet, of course."

"My dad never mentioned it. That you're on the big job."

Brendon stopped mixing mayonnaise into tuna fish. "Does that bother you?"

"Not really, no. And I haven't dealt with the business for some time now, so why would he tell me? By the way, one of the jobs I'm working on is a company that's developing a toilet that uses no water. It's all biodegradable."

"Sounds like science fiction. And I thought your work was top secret."

"It is, but we just approved them. It'll be in the news before long."

"I'll believe it when it puts me out of business."

"It's meant for marginalized communities, so don't worry, your career's safe."

Brendon finished assembling the sandwiches, cutting them in half and tossing potato chips on both plates. Having fetched the sodas, Peppa joined him at the table. They sat side by side, looking through the window toward Maloney's house of crime.

"This view. Two chairs. A blanket. The good life!" she said, giggling.

"The only thing left to make it complete paradise is a toilet. Maybe I should buy one of those inventions."

"The thing's huge. It'd never fit past the door."

"Ah well, I'll live."

While Brendon plowed through his sandwich, Peppa scraped the tuna fish from between the bread slices with a fork and took a few bites. There was a funny taste to it. Slightly sour.

"You're not hungry at all?" he asked.

"I usually skip lunch on the weekends."

"But it's almost four . . . you could call this an early dinner."

"Can we drop it?"

"Okay, but—"

"*Please*?" She looked at the ceiling. The surface was that popcorn application. Who invented such an awful thing? Peppa closed her eyes. There was the bench, burned into her eyelids. She could smell the salt water. "That topic. Food? Not a word," she said.

"Done. Wanna pick something from the list?"

They looked at it together and simultaneously pointed to the same thing. *Read Virginia aloud*. He reached over to the end of the table and grabbed *A Writer's Diary*.

"Let's do this one first," he said. "I bought all her novels too. Figured I might as well since I'm flush at the moment."

"How about this for an idea," Peppa said. "Since it's not a novel, let's open to a random page and read two or three sentences. We'll alternate."

"Really? Kind of disorganized, don't you think?"

"Well, there're gaps in time between the entries, so the narrative's not really connected. Can we at least try it?"

"Sure. Could be cool."

Peppa took the book from him and ran her fingers over the embossed lettering. He'd purchased a hardcover. Then she looked at the stack of Virginia's novels on the floor across the room. All hardcovers. During the phone calls, they'd cooked up this project of reading all of Virginia's books aloud to each other. It would take a very long time, a detail both of them avoided pointing out. But now she saw that he'd spent precious money, essentially investing in their future. Peppa closed her eyes again. This time she saw her red Christmas coat floating in the water. And the sour taste was still there, more than ever. She should have eaten the bread. Something to absorb the putrid fish and disgusting mayo.

"Is your stomach off from the tuna?" she asked.

"No. I'm fine."

"Then it must be me. Okay, I guess I'll start."

She opened the book and let the pages flip slowly. She found herself trying to catch phrases that might have substance. About Virginia's marriage or her publishing successes. Big topics and important moments. But then she stopped herself. *Random* meant no forethought, in the moment. So Peppa closed the book and re-opened it, then stabbed at some words and read.

"'To lie on the sofa for a week. I am sitting up today in the usual state of unequal animation. But I doubt that I can write to any purpose.'"

"I don't like this one," she said. "Can I try another?"

"Yes, of course."

She skipped to the middle of the book and read from the top of the left page.

"'All desire to practice the art of a writer has completely left. I cannot imagine what it would be like: that is, more accurately, I cannot curve my mind to the line of a book.'"

"This one's bad too. Maybe if I read more toward the beginning, it'll be more cheerful."

"That makes sense."

She opened to the very front of the book and read from the bottom of the right page.

"'Then I begin to wonder what it is that I am doing; to suspect, as is usual in such cases, that I have not thought my plan out plainly enough . . . which means that one is lost.'"

"Oh, God. Why am I picking these awful passages?"

"Try it again," he said. "You'll find the right one."

"Okay, just one more, I promise."

Now she flipped all the pages back and forth several times as a kind of clearing. Then she noticed that a page had been dog-eared. "Did you start this already?"

"No. Maybe it happened in the bookstore. Someone browsed and tagged the page?"

"Or maybe the dog-ear is a sign."

"Like an omen?"

"But aren't they bad?"

"Omens can be one way or the other," he said.

"No. It can't be a fifty-fifty thing."

"But you've picked three bad passages. The odds are in your favor that the next one will be more cheerful."

"Okay, that sounds plausible. But Brendon, do *you* think I should try the words on the dog-eared page?"

He thrummed his fingers on the table. "I do."

"And do you truly believe the omen will be the good kind?"

"I can't say for sure, but things seem to be pointing in that direction."

The dog-eared page number was 318. She raised her eyes up from the number to the halfway point and read from the beginning of the paragraph.

"'I would like to tell myself a nice little improbable story to spread my wings after the cramped ant-like morning — which I will not detail — for details are the death of me.'"

"Oh no. I'm sorry," Brendon whispered.

Peppa's mom always used that exact phrase—*details are the death of me*—especially when she went off her meds. It was a verbal tic signaling that she was about to fall into a bad episode and possibly disappear.

And Peppa thought, *Dear Virginia, please, please don't be like my mom.*

"Virginia was really quite sad, wasn't she?" Brendon said after some time.

"She had episodes most of her life."

"Piled heavy stones in her pockets to die in some river, was it?"

"It's awful when your mind tells you what to do and there's no way to stop it."

"Should I have my turn now?" he asked. "Or we could lie on the bed. Rest a bit."

Peppa placed Virginia's diary on the table and sat on the bed. She kicked off her shoes and slipped under the covers with her clothes on. Brendon dug in behind, gathering her to him. They stayed very still for quite some time. When she turned around, he wasn't smiling. This was the first good thing that had happened that day. Like GoGo said, it felt as if Brendon was seeing her.

"It'll be all right, Peppa," Brendon said.

"How do you know?"

"I just do."

Peppa closed her eyes and saw the seashells.

A VERY GOOD BRAIN

SHE PULLED A FLIMSY ROBE TIGHT AROUND HER BODY AND RETIED THE WAIST string. Her legs dangled off the table. Shivering hard, she stuck her hands between her thighs for warmth, then rubbed an itch on her nose with her shoulder. Her armpits smelled something awful. It had taken Peppa many weeks to finally admit to the reason she needed to be here, sitting in this particular office on a metal table with stirrups at one end. There were so many ways her mom had failed her, though Peppa was never allowed to cast blame because her mom, after all, was and always had been the more important victim. In their family the talking points were *she can't help it*, *she's not in control*, and *it's not her fault*, all of which Peppa would never deny. But this—sitting almost naked in an over-air-conditioned examining room—*this* was all her mom's fault. Every bit of it.

Peppa had never gotten the "talk" other than being told not to be frightened of menstrual blood because it was *for her baby*. A perplexing and scary notion at the age of twelve. But she eventually weeded out the facts from fairy tales by eavesdropping on the gossip in school bathrooms. By twelfth grade, she had the story more or less down, though she doubted she'd ever need, or want, to perform the various activities and techniques described. Then, when she started working for Ivan, her mom revisited the subject and dragged her to their crotchety seventy-year-old family doctor to be fitted for a diaphragm. And she insisted Peppa carry the thing with her every single hour, seven days a week. Her mom believed that Manhattan was a dangerous slum, filled with on-the-prowl rapists, perverts, and subnorms. Not to mention those inflicted with contagions like conjunctivitis and crotch rot. To anyone other than her mom, Peppa would have pointed out that if she *was* assaulted, the guy wouldn't wait for her to dig through her purse and shove the diaphragm into place. But explaining reasonable assumptions of human behavior, however criminal, did not align with her mom's bizarre view of the world.

And how terribly *unfair* her predicament was, Peppa thought. Because wasn't she just one of the millions of girls who forgot about birth control their first time? And wasn't it then reasonable to expect that at the least, a slim majority of them would come through it unscathed? In her case, the act had been so unexpected it made total sense that she hadn't given a thought to the diaphragm zippered into a secret pocket in her purse less than a foot from Brendon's bed. Anyway, she couldn't imagine anyone *planning* virgin sex, discussing the day, the location, even what to wear. And if her experience with Brendon had been in any way typical, stopping mid-action was next to impossible because she'd been in the throes, as she imagined Virginia might say.

She heard footsteps from the other side of the door. Expecting someone to enter, Peppa palmed tears from her cheeks and inhaled a shuddery breath. But whoever it was walked further down the hall and entered the room next to hers. Through the wall, the conversation sounded like friends catching up—happy women jabbering back and forth. Maybe this woman had a husband. Maybe she was on her third kid. Maybe they'd planned all three pregnancies. Regardless, it was obvious the woman hadn't suffered any recent lapses of judgment, because now they were laughing. Peppa hadn't laughed since she realized her period, which usually arrived as predictably as the sun and the moon, was a no-show. And while she kept upbeat with Ivan and GoGo and avoided her parents, crying—when she was alone in her bedroom, alone in a toilet stall at LBS, alone in the cab to and from work—provided only fleeting relief.

But yesterday, late in the day when her stoicism had weakened, Ivan caught Peppa at her desk, silent-sobbing into her hands. In less than a minute, he pried the truth from her, after which Peppa bawled openly, grateful that finally someone knew. Ivan insisted they all go to dinner to talk it through, and GoGo scored a coveted corner table at the Union Square Café. During the meal, they gently chided her for not telling them sooner and, since they'd not yet met Brendon, were eager to schedule an inspection. They assumed that Peppa would marry him. And they drilled further down into other fantasies too, like wondering whether the baby could have two godfathers. She wept on and off throughout because, while it sounded like a perfectly fine future for anyone other than her, she knew what she must do.

By the time the check was paid, Ivan had reached a close female associate who prevailed upon her high-end ob-gyn boyfriend. An appointment was confirmed before they climbed into their respective cabs. On the ride home, Peppa thought about how her friends had dropped everything for her. They had opera tickets to a sold-out run at the Met that night but didn't care at all about missing it. These were two good men and they were on her wall. But as much as they'd tried to buoy her spirits by assuring her that *everything would work out* and *what a wonderful mother she'd make*, when she walked into her house, their optimism went poof. Peppa knew she was doomed.

Finally, the doctor and his nurse entered. He looked annoyed, but the nurse seemed kind of upbeat. Couldn't they at least get their affects coordinated?

"Sorry for the delay, Ms. Ryan," the doctor said. "We were waiting for your records to be faxed over from your family physician."

"Oh God. He's a lunatic."

"He seemed lucid enough when I spoke with him on the phone."

"You didn't tell him, did you?"

"Of course not." He flipped through some papers. "Okay. Twenty years old. And you've not been pregnant before."

"No. I mean, that's correct."

"Any health problems at the moment?"

"None."

"I see from your last checkup a year ago your weight was 120."

Peppa shook her head. "No. No way."

"That's wrong?"

"Yeah, nowhere near correct. That guy's scale is a mess. I've got to be around 135. Probably more."

"Our scale puts you at 124, but no matter. Your blood draw confirmed that you are pregnant." He paused. "Congratulations."

Peppa's head dropped. The next sound she heard was the nurse clearing her throat.

"Want to tell us what's going on?" she asked.

"I'm not married. I'm doomed."

"Not necessarily," the doctor said.

Peppa gave him an exasperated look as if to say *what do you know?*

"There are a number of options," he continued. "However, according to the intake form, you're toward the end of the first trimester. I'll have to confirm that with an ultrasound, of course, but if you decide to terminate, it should be soon. Waiting becomes riskier for a variety of reasons."

The sour expression on his face hadn't budged. Why was this guy delivering babies? He should have been a podiatrist—corns and bunions and the like. But he was probably just irritable because his girlfriend made him squeeze her in.

"Okay, Ms. Ryan. I was happy to fit you in this morning, but I have another patient I need to see."

She jumped off the table. "Right. I'd better get going too."

"I'm not kicking you out."

"Oh. I kind of thought you were."

"Not at all. I was about to suggest that you discuss this more thoroughly with my nurse. Linda will give you all the information. And take as much time as you need."

Once the doctor left, Nurse Linda handed her two more thin blankets. "I know it's cold in here."

Peppa draped one across her legs, the other around her shoulders. "Your boss doesn't smile."

"He's just busy. Do you know who the father is?"

"What kind of question is that? Of course."

"It's the first one I always ask unmarried women. It's best not to assume anything."

"Oh . . . right," Peppa said.

"Is he a steady boyfriend?"

"Kind of."

"Does he know?"

Peppa shook her head.

"What about anyone in your family?" the nurse asked.

"My parents are Irish Catholic and pretty conservative. They'd freak if they knew we had sex."

"You don't think they suspect or maybe even assume?"

"God no. Never."

"A best girlfriend?"

"Only my boss and his boyfriend know. I told them yesterday."

"Okay, I've got some literature about your options." Nurse Linda slid a folder onto Peppa's lap. "This way you'll be well informed when you do speak with your boyfriend."

The folder looked way too thick and felt much too heavy. How many options could there be? She'd already thought about and discarded the obvious ones. Her parents would definitely agree to take the kid on, but only if she'd make believe it was theirs and act thrilled to finally have a sibling. Or, if she decided to raise it, they'd freak out due to Catholic shame and kick her out of the house. Then she'd lose her job with Ivan and end up raising the kid on welfare. But the worst was a shotgun wedding to Brendon. They'd be miserable from the jump. She'd nag him into multiple affairs and eventually alcoholism.

One day the earth splits apart; I fall into the crevasse. The next, I observe a very strange bird I've not noticed till now, which is news I'll be eager to tell Leonard about.

On rare occasions, Virginia disappointed Peppa with optimism.

"Listen, I'm sure you have better things to do." Peppa jumped off the table again. The blankets puddled to the floor and the robe fell from her shoulder, exposing her swollen breasts. After Nurse Linda pulled the robe up, her hand settled on Peppa's arm.

"This is important. Don't you think? Stay."

Peppa was due to meet Ivan and GoGo for lunch at Le Bernardin in an hour. She figured killing time here was as good a place as any. "Can I at least get dressed?"

"Of course."

She quickly pulled on her clothes and jumped back onto the examining table. Nurse Linda canted her body against a counter and winked.

"What?" Peppa asked warily.

"I've seen a lot of women go through this."

"You have?"

"Part of what's happening is that you've kept it to yourself, and I can understand why you'd feel the need to do that. Now it's built up in your mind. But once you have all the information, you might be surprised how things go."

Peppa had no response to what sounded like bullet points from a nursing school's do's-and-don'ts list: *Do* try to put the patient at ease, even though she's actually doomed.

"Are you and your boyfriend committed to each other?" Nurse Linda asked.

"We got together only a couple of months ago."

"But he cares about you?"

"Yes."

"Tell me about him."

"Really?"

"Why not?"

"He's decent looking," Peppa said. "So . . . I'm lucky that way."

"You're quite beautiful. I'm sure he feels the same."

Ivan told lies too, when clients needed to be plumped up with flattery. Peppa waited a few seconds for her irritation to subside.

"What about the work you both do?"

"I'm in finance. He's a plumber. My parents own a construction business and he's been working for them. That's how we met."

"What do you do for fun?"

"Well, we like books."

"What kind?"

"The classics mostly," Peppa said. "We're reading to each other. Out loud."

"Huh. That's really cool."

"Yeah, it's been nice."

"Okay. I know this is a new relationship, but have you talked at all with your boyfriend about the future? Even in general terms."

"There're problems back in Ireland, where he's from. And to be honest, I'm not sure he'll even stay in the States."

"But the point is, you're pregnant. And whatever you decide to do, you'll need to tell him. Talk it out. The best option will become clear. I promise you."

Nurse Linda had just lost her last shred of cred. Peppa had no intention of talking it out, so why even tell him in the first place? And *clarity* was code for *start praying because you are doomed.* She had to get out of this dreadful office and far away from this awful memorizer of nursing school nonsense. She jumped off the table for the final time, leaving the thick folder behind.

Once outside, Peppa speed-walked north to Central Park South. And like an omen, the good kind, there they were: horse-drawn buggies. Just like the ones Virginia rode in London. She found an empty bench, and a driver approached her for business. She brushed him off before he got too deep into his pitch. But then a new option occurred to her. She would ditch Le Bernardin altogether and ride through Central Park in a carriage. She could picture Virginia in an ankle-length green velvet dress and a brimmed hat for shade, doing just exactly this—listening to the clip-clop of hooves, smelling the oiled-leather seat, feeling a scratchy blanket on her knees. Now Peppa looked around for the hack, but he was long gone, so she beckoned to the driver who was next in line. He looked her over and quoted five hundred dollars for the day. Peppa laughed. He immediately reduced it by four hundred. She searched in her purse but could produce only a single twenty. Now he laughed and walked away. She closed her eyes, and instead of seeing things that reminded her of the blind game, she was relieved to see only the back of her eyelids. Another good omen.

Then she felt a sharp surge of . . . *something*. It began in her toes, drilled up through her body, landed at the base of her neck, then stayed there and throbbed. The sensation was entirely unfamiliar. But it wasn't awful.

Her phone rang. "Oh, Ivan! I'll be there in five minutes."

"We were worried," he said.

"No, I'm good."

"Okay, what should I order for you?"

"Ummm . . . that appetizer. Scallops."

"That's all?"

"Yeah, for now. I'm getting a cab."

It had begun to rain. Taxis whizzed by, occupied. A buggy pulled up and unloaded a family of five. She told the driver the address and waved the twenty-dollar bill. Peppa knew bringing the horse into traffic wasn't legal, but this driver didn't hesitate. He dragged the overhang up and tossed a blanket over her lap. As he pulled away from the curb and aimed the horse in the direction of Le Bernardin, she believed the rattle of the buggy's wheels on the rough pavement sounded exactly like the cobblestones of London during Virginia's time. The best omen yet.

Dear Virginia, Peppa thought, *do you know about the good omens too?*

She found GoGo and Ivan sitting at the very back of the restaurant. She slipped into the chair between them, and Ivan poured sparkling water. Peppa gulped the entire glass, half of it dribbling down her chin.

"My dear *girl*. Here, let me mop that up," GoGo said, dabbing at her with a napkin. "You're so late. What have you been doing?"

"I was in the park. I guess I lost track of the time."

"Well, eat the scallops before they go completely cold," Ivan said. "We just ordered dessert, but I'll tell the waiter to hold off until you're done."

"No, let him bring it. I'm not sure I can keep food down. Anyway, we have to get back to the office soon, right? That conference call at two."

"I cancelled it."

"Why?"

"We're not going back to the office. This is too important."

"I'm perfectly capable of carrying on with the day. Everything as usual."

"Based on your current predicament and your behavior yesterday, things are not exactly usual," Ivan said.

"I had a cry. So?"

His eyebrow levitated.

"Okay, a couple of jags," she said.

"If that's how you need to frame it, fine. But we're taking over. GoGo. Tell her."

"You're to stay with us," GoGo said. "At the apartment."

"What do you mean? *Live* with you?" Peppa asked.

"Exactly. It'll be fun. Like an endless sleepover."

"Okay, wait a minute. You can't spring this on me."

"But it's all set," GoGo said. "Last night we got the guest suite plumped and primped. You'll spend hours lying around staring at the clouds. I find them depressing, but I know how devoted you are to them. You can even take time off from work."

"C'mon, you guys. I don't have consumption. I'm pregnant."

"Also, I've ordered Frette bed linens with periwinkles bordering the edges. Cheerful. Right, Ivan?"

"They're okay."

"This is for *Peppa*. Can you just agree with me?"

"They're fine," Ivan said.

"And, I bought some lavender lotion made from the fat of curly horned goats who live not far from Giverny. Monet must have used them as inspiration—"

Ivan broke in. "GoGo, please. Try very hard not to regress. Peppa, as usual, GoGo is light-years ahead. I was going to bring all this up after you told us about the doctor visit. But we do think it wise for you to stay with us."

"Maybe. Can I think about it?"

"Of course. But what happened with the doctor?"

"He was kind of annoying. The nurse tried to be all nice and sincere, giving me options. But I'm pretty sure I'm going to kill it."

Ivan grabbed her hand and squeezed it. She shook him off and pointed to the pumpkin mousse the waiter had just delivered. "Go ahead. Dig in. And wow—look at that dollop of whipped cream. Now that's a work of art. It reminds me of the first time we came here. Remember?"

She looked down at her plate and began talking directly to her scallops, because they would really understand her. "That writer chef—Tony something—didn't show. Anyway, I think these guys had steaks, and I had risotto. And I remember the three of us shared a Caesar salad to save room for this *exact* dessert. I was sure I'd hate it. But they insisted I at least try. And it was delicious. I mean, I *loved* that mousse."

Now she looked up and saw that neither Ivan nor GoGo had taken a spoonful of the mousse. "What are you waiting for? *Eat.*"

She returned to her scallops. "But that day. I was already pregnant, because the weekend before was when I met Brendon. And now these guys love each other. But I really don't know what I'm going to do about Brendon. Because he's going to leave me. And there's lots and lots of reasons why he *should* leave me. But I can't have it be because of the baby."

Peppa paused, then nodded vigorously at her plate. "Yes, you're right. Nurse Linda did say that I have options. But the doctor said if I want to do *that* option, I should do it soon. So I've sorted the details in my head. I'll be out of work for two days. I won't tell a soul. Not my parents. Not Brendon." Her hand dropped to her belly. Then she shook her head at the scallops. "No. You're wrong. He *will* leave me. But it can't be because of this. Not the baby."

"Oh, sweetie," Ivan whispered.

She looked up. The restaurant was full. People were eating like hogs. Drinking like camels. The lighting seemed to bounce off every metal surface in the room. Now the *something* sensation was back. It moved around from the back of her neck to her throat. Peppa closed her eyes and didn't like what she saw. The bench.

To move forward feels useless; trivial. Perhaps dangerous.

She shoved the plate of scallops to the middle of the table, knocking the bread basket onto the floor. "Ivan, listen to me," Peppa said. "I want to go backwards. To when I first came to work for you. Remember? You understood me. You trusted me. And you said our work could change the world. I want to do that. Only that. I don't want a plumber in my life. I don't want a plumber's baby inside me. I don't want to raise a plumber's baby. I only want to use my brain . . . Ivan? I have a *good* brain. Right?"

"Yes, Peppa. A very good brain."

They convinced her to come to the apartment for the rest of the afternoon. When they arrived, Peppa headed directly for the sofa. She grabbed a blanket draped over the back and bundled up. She was hoping for the distraction of clouds to take her mind off the source of her disquiet, but the sky had cleared up. And now the color blue made her weep.

She gripped her belly, and the baby, and thought, *Dear Virginia, help me.*

Ivan and GoGo bustled in with a tray of tea and shortbread cookies and sat on either side of Peppa. She leaned over and continued to sob into GoGo's neck. Shortly, he wiped the tears under each eye with his thumb and offered her a cookie. "Want this?"

She plucked it from his hand and nibbled while looking around. "I haven't been here for a few weeks. A coffee table. A rug. You're ahead of schedule, Ivan." She tested a smile, hoping to clear the air of their concern.

Ivan ran his hand across the table. "Yes, it's pretty."

"Very. So nice. Oh God, *no*," she said as the tears threatened to return. She squeezed her hands into fists until the urge subsided.

Ivan sidled closer. "Peppa, tell me you're not going crazy."

"What? I'm fine. Why would you even say that?"

"Because you're going from a hundred to zero and back."

"Don't worry. I'm in total control."

"But I do worry. None of this makes any sense. We assumed you were still seeing Brendon, but you didn't mention him again after that day with the Toilets. Then we find out you've been pregnant this entire time. And now you plan to abort your baby."

"It's the option I've chosen," she explained with prim defiance. "And it's the right one."

"Okay, that may end up being the case. But what you haven't mentioned at all is Brendon. Other than to say he's going to leave you."

Peppa handed the half-eaten cookie to GoGo. "I can't bear this. You eat it."

"Does he love you?" Ivan asked.

She winced. "Once he called me *his treasure*, but in Gaelic."

"How bizarre," GoGo whispered.

"GoGo, please, no commentary," Ivan said. "Peppa, I know you're scared. And that's normal. Who wouldn't be? And we very much want to help. But I know there's a lot you're not telling us."

"I'm supposed to see him tonight."

"So you can tell him then. Right?"

"That I'm going to get rid of it."

"God, Peppa," Ivan said. "You absolutely cannot say anything like that without first simply telling him you're pregnant. You have to see what his reaction is. He'll have feelings about it."

"Like, happy or sad?"

"I suspect it won't be that cut and dried."

"Maybe not," she agreed.

"But be fair. You need to give him time to absorb the news."

"So, let me get this straight. You're saying I can do what I want as long as I tell him about the baby and let him have his feelings."

"And you need to *consider* his feelings."

"Okay. I'll consider them."

"It's a conversation," Ivan said. "A back-and-forth. And remain open."

"Sure. Open."

"C'mon, Peppa. Don't play games."

"I promise."

And Peppa thought, *Dear Virginia, do you always tell the truth?*

DEAR VIRGINIA, WAIT FOR ME

PEPPA'S MOM STOOD IN THE FOYER OF THEIR HOUSE, LOOKING MORE PUT-together than usual. She wore a simple shirtwaist dress, a style that suited her slim figure. Also, a fairly successful attempt at makeup. Peppa figured something must have happened for her to have spent more than three seconds on appearance, let alone get out of her bathrobe. But since she hadn't eaten anything at lunch and only one half of a cookie at Ivan's, an honest hunger killed any further curiosity. She kicked the front door shut and blew past her mom, aiming for the first thing she saw in the fridge. A jumble of chicken legs were glued to a platter. She pried four off the stack and devoured them. Napping on the bus ride home seemed to have made food desirable, and the idea of normal conversation plausible. And now she also noticed that the *something* was gone.

"You're home early. Something the matter?" her mom asked after Peppa finished two more legs.

"I was . . . it was . . . slow," Peppa said, wiping grease from her chin with her palm. "Ivan sent me home."

"Well, I'm glad to know he's got at least half a heart."

"He's not the type of boss who makes me punch a time clock. If there's nothing to do, I leave. But that rarely happens."

"I've noticed."

"Mother, what's the problem? Do we really need to rehash your disapproval of my work?"

"You have a boyfriend now."

"You'll be disappointed to know that Brendon actually admires the fact that I'm committed to what I do. Just as I'm sure you're thrilled that he's keen on becoming the most successful plumber that ever lived. And we'd both like to manage our careers without interference. If that's okay with you, that is," Peppa said.

"Far be it from me to stop you from carrying on like a headless robot. But your father thinks a balance is necessary."

"Oh please. I walk in the door and immediately get fed a bunch of work/life advice. And from *Dad* of all people? No thank you." Peppa threw the bones into the garbage can, then noticed their best china stacked in the sink. Due to her mom's non-existent housekeeping skills, the roach population would enjoy an overnight meal, so Peppa set to washing the dishes. "Looks like you had yourself a little party today," she said, filling the sink with hot water.

"Not a party."

"What then?"

"Your father and I had Brendon over for tea."

The *something* surged back, this time right behind Peppa's eyes. "What in the bloody hell!" she yelled, throwing a sopping wet dishrag across the room. The rag splatted against the wall and slithered to the floor.

"We're your parents."

"And your point?"

"We felt it necessary to understand his intentions," Patrice said.

"Whose idea was this? Must have been Daddy."

"Both of us."

"But we've been dating only a short time. Couldn't you at least have waited until we'd gotten past our first fight?" Peppa grabbed the rag off the floor. It stank. She tossed it in the garbage can. "Just out of curiosity, when was this arranged?"

"Last week."

"He didn't say anything about it to me."

"We asked him not to."

"My God. You've got my boyfriend deceiving me?"

"Don't make a federal case, Peppa."

"Fine. I'm supposed to see him tonight for our book thing. Now I'm gonna cancel."

"Don't."

"Why not? You're ruining everything."

"He cares about you," Patrice said.

"I don't need you to tell me whether or not he cares. Look, Mother. You were the one who begged me to see him. Just once. Remember that? And now you and Dad want to see if he's suitable enough to continue dating me?"

"You're twisting this."

"And you're interfering!" Peppa yelled.

Her mom shrugged. "What would you have us do? You tell us absolutely nothing."

The chicken legs sat in Peppa's belly, just above the baby. And the *something* had traveled down to the same location. She couldn't tell which of the three was causing her to feel so nauseated. "Say I went to Brendon's tonight as planned. Am I supposed to know about this meet and greet?"

"We asked that it stay between the three of us."

"And he was okay with that?"

"Seemed to be," Patrice said.

This was getting really confusing. "Then why are you telling me?"

"You deserve to know. Woman to woman."

"Spare me your liberation, Mother. How long was he here?"

"Maybe . . . two hours?"

"You're lucky I didn't come home sooner."

"But you didn't."

Peppa sat at the table. If this was the way it was going to play out, everybody knowing everything about a supposed secret meeting, she might as well dig for details. "So, what did he say?"

Her mom looked at the light bulb hanging from the ceiling, her favorite beacon when she needed to phrase something in a particular way. Peppa braced.

"He likes you a lot."

"That's it?"

"Well, a little more than that."

"Don't make me pry this out of you," Peppa said.

"He thinks he might be in love."

"*Thinks*? *Might*? Sounds like a dodge."

"Okay, the phrase was . . . *Peppa is a lovable woman.*"

"That's a dodge. It's floating in space. He doesn't attach it to himself," Peppa said. Her mom didn't have a comeback, which meant she agreed. "So, in that entire time, that's all you got out of him? That I am, somewhere in the vast universe, lovable."

"If he professed undying love, that would have raised a flag. At least for me. But the chat was short, less than ten minutes. He and your father had a lot to discuss about all the jobs he's on, so I went upstairs to take a nap. I woke just as they were leaving. Your father had to pick up supplies at the Home Depot."

"Did he go with him?"

"Daughter, it's after four, not my best time of day. Don't tromp on the weeds. We're satisfied with the young man."

They were satisfied, and it surprised Peppa how relieved she was that they were. And regardless of the remote possibility that she and Brendon would end up together, let alone raise a baby, she did agree with their decision to avoid an awkward foursome where nothing remotely honest could have been extracted from him, or her.

"Peppa, go check the ledger for me. Make sure the sums are in order. I've handed over the bookkeeping to your father."

"Oh. I didn't know that, Mom."

"He insisted. And it's for the best."

"Okay. But how far back should I go?"

"You just ate all our leftovers. Now I've got to get a meal sorted. You'll know what to do."

Peppa entered the office and shut the door. It felt like a prison: closed in and tragic. She didn't see the ledger, which was usually on the computer desk to the right of the keyboard. Instead, a mound of papers covered the surface. She and her mom had for many years tag-teamed, working the ledger with impeccable accuracy. It was a strange, yet necessary connection that Peppa missed in this moment. She'd see what her mom had entered and could oftentimes glean her state of mind from whether or not the handwriting was legible. If it wasn't, she knew that her mom had likely gone off the pills, and Peppa would then be on alert for a possible event.

Now she began to snoop for the ledger in earnest. She opened and closed several drawers. Then she dug under the papers, being careful not to disturb the pile too much because the mess usually had some manner of cryptic organization to it. Nothing there. She turned and scanned the entire room in hopes the glossy black cover would simply pop up and show itself. That's when she saw that the office had been rearranged. Their ancient metal cabinets were shoved up against one wall which created, for the first time ever, a decent amount of empty floor space. And new cardboard storage boxes were stacked and labeled with thick red lettering. Clearly, this was a more-than-decent attempt at the inventory taking she'd been hounding her parents about for the longest time. The smell of mold was gone too. When had all of this happened? Oddly, she felt left out. Which was ridiculous. These stabs at their independence were exactly what she'd been hoping for.

Now she saw Brendon's sweater draped over the back of a chair tucked under, not a piece of junk, but a brand-new table. It was the same sweater he'd wrapped around her naked shoulders their first time together.

I've no ability to identify treachery disguised within the mundane.

Dear Virginia, Peppa thought, *he left the sweater after the meeting. Don't worry so much.*

Peppa sat down and pushed her arms into the sweater, his distinct odor still very present. She could picture Brendon and her dad sitting at this table, discussing the jobs, talking through scheduling, and it wasn't such a bad image. Then it occurred to her that since Brendon was working so much, maybe he'd be able to raise the money for his sister. And if she got better and even survived the cancer entirely, then he could stay in the States. Also, according to her mom, Brendon considered her lovable. And while not the exact phrasing she'd hoped for, somehow those words were good enough. For her, and perhaps the baby too.

With all this dreamy realignment of her future, Peppa had missed the main attraction. The ledger, obscured due to a shadow created by the new stack of boxes, was at the far end of the table. She pulled it closer and ran her hand over the gold-tone embossed words. *Ryan Irish Construction.* The silk ribbon slithered loose from the top of the ledger like a long worm. Not, as her mom preferred, secured between the pages of the most recent entries. This was her dad's typical carelessness, and Peppa smiled at the thought. She opened to the first page, the date from about five months ago. There were notes in the margin about things her mom wanted Peppa to do. *Call Home Depot about refund. Pay electrician for extra work.* And funny that she remembered those exact reminders and also making the call and cutting the check. Then she turned several more pages and was startled to see *Brendon Maloney*, his name written with her mom's unique hand. The date was from about a week before Peppa and Brendon met, likely the day of the Maloney bridal shower. Peppa had been working with Ivan for some time at that point and wasn't attending to the ledger anymore. So it made sense that she'd never seen this.

She leafed through more pages until the color red popped out: $5,000, in her dad's scrawl. The date was about three months ago, but no attribution as to the recipient. From the time Peppa was taught to work the books, there had never been any color other than soft black pencil. On instinct, she flipped to the most recent entry. Today's date. $10,000. Again, in her dad's hand. Now Peppa leafed through all the previous pages, red popping out everywhere like a flip-book animation with no obvious story. Who was getting paid such huge sums of money?

She pulled the storage box marked *CHECKS* to the middle of the room and grabbed the closest stack, held together with a loose rubber band. Thumbing through, she added the numbers in her head.

$90,000. Paid to the order of Brendon Maloney.

The *something*, still close to her baby, began to pulse.

I have the doom on my mind; I daresay, it cleaves.

Oh no, Virginia.

They were paying the plumber to date her. Marry her. Produce grandchildren.

Peppa walked to the cluttered desk. Screaming from a sea of white was the red pencil. She grabbed it, then swept the papers to the floor. They resettled into a fresh pile she hoped her mom and dad would never be able to sort out. Then she placed the ledger, the stack of cancelled checks, and the red pencil on the empty surface. She played with these objects, shifting them from here to there, not yet sure of what she wanted to do or even how she wished things would go. Then she noticed that the ledger and the checks were exactly the same length. She angled the edges to make two equal sides of a triangle. If this was to be a good omen, the red pencil would create her favorite equilateral triangle. She quickly slid it into place.

The triangle was obtuse. Dull. Stupid. And a very bad omen.

When Peppa opened the door to the kitchen, her mom was pressing meat into a skillet on the stove with a spatula.

"It's all fine, Mom."

"Well, that's a first. Your father's math."

Peppa forced a smile. "Right."

"What's that you're wearing?"

"It's Brendon's. He must have left it. I'm going there now. *A Room of One's Own*. Virginia Woolf."

"Sounds just glorious."

Peppa hated her mom's sarcasm.

And now the *something* shot to her knees and made them buckle.

She steadied herself at the wall.

"Peppa? What's wrong?"

"Just hungry, I guess. Brendon will have food waiting for me. I'll be late."

She stood outside at the end of the front walk for several minutes. The sun was about to set, and the temperature was cooler than expected. She'd neglected to grab a coat and considered going back for it. But Brendon's sweater had a hood, so she flipped it over her head and buttoned up. Maloneys' house was down the block to her left, and she could see the garage roof from this vantage point. And the light coming from Brendon's room. She turned right.

She found the bench. And it was, for certain, the bench. She sat, and still feeling destabilized, gripped the edge to keep from falling forward. Then, the *something* engulfed her body entirely.

I've never understood the advantage, or even the use, of vague language. Linear thought, or better, a summary, at times serves an obvious purpose.

Yes, Virginia.

All this time, the plumber's lies had flowed from his mouth, slippery and smooth. His insistence that she was *gorgeous* and had what he called a body that *killed*. But no wonder he was shifty about the love. Because the plumber was a fraud or, as her dad used to call subcontractors when they stiffed him, a bad actor. And now she suspected he'd been playing the role of a plumber. She had never seen a single tool of his trade in that room—not a wrench or a snake. And unlike every plumber she'd ever known, whose hands she never wanted to shake because yuck, Brendon's fingernails were always clean and manicured. And his too-soft hands, as if they'd never been within ten miles of a New York City gut job. Then, the saintly sister. Supposedly filled to the brim with tumors. It was a really good plotline, because who would ever question the holy grail of excuses for everything under the sun—a cancer diagnosis.

Rearing children may result in less than optimal results; due to neglect, or much worse.

Suddenly, the *something* gathered itself up and shot like a bullet into her head. And now Peppa remembered more of that day. Her mom, stretching out underneath the bench, coaxing Peppa to lie face-up on top of her, to be her blanket, to keep her warm. Which she did, and for a long time. Then her mom's hands, like claws, restraining her from escaping, telling Peppa to close her eyes and play the blind game. To imagine not being under the bench, to pretend she was somewhere else, to make believe she wasn't cold. Then, after the longest time, Peppa giving up on the blind game and opening her eyes. Staring through the slats. Seeing that the sky had turned black. Noticing that her body had gone numb. And then, nothing after that.

Well; the cleaving is done.

Oh God, Virginia.

Peppa began to search, but this time without a need for perfection. She circled and circled and circled the bench. Grabbing any seashells she could find, but mostly sand, she stuffed her pockets. When she felt heavy enough, she spread the plumber's sweater beneath the bench. She lay on top and knotted the arms tight around her baby. She briefly thought of her mom, then closed her eyes and played the blind game for the last time. Before long, a chill assembled around her, and she imagined that the sun was now gone. Later, she felt a strong breeze blow across her body. Then, when the *something* had subsided to almost nothing, Peppa knew that something else was very near. And now all that was left for her to do was to sink into this blackness, this place where there were no betrayals. No plumber. And no longer a need to decide anything at all about her baby.

And Peppa thought, *I'm almost there. Dear Virginia, wait for me.*

YELLOW

Yellow had never been her color. Especially now at the facility, because it made her think of things she had no access to, such as the taxicabs that took her to work and back home. And just her luck that the room she'd been assigned to had a wide yellow stripe running horizontally around the space, including across the door. Peppa felt corralled by the color yellow. And there were no pictures on the walls, nothing to break up the monotony of the white above and below the yellow stripe. Even the round wall clock had been removed because of her propensity to fixate on geometrics. And so the only way to gauge the passage of time was when someone broke through the yellow on the door to deliver food and pills several times a day. In this way, Peppa realized that the yellow was necessary as a way of telling the difference between morning and noon, or twilight and night. In fact, she eventually came to see yellow as a good omen. Because the people who broke through the yellow stripe were actually really nice. And she *was* able to see the yellow sun from the high window for a few hours each morning, which cheered her up. Then, one day, Peppa found herself missing the outside world, and Dr. Welsh announced she'd had a mini breakthrough. She told him it was because of the color yellow.

At first, she didn't like Dr. Welsh at all. He seemed committed to never reacting to anything she said. And then out of nowhere, a kind of falling in love happened, which he assured her was perfectly normal—something called transference. He also cautioned her that at some point she'd probably hate him. And that happened too. Whatever her flip-flopping, five times a week Dr. Welsh poked at her psyche with a tiny bit of Freud, a fair amount of Jungian dream analysis, classic early childhood theories of Margaret Mahler, and the magnum opus of mother-daughter hell—object relations theory. And while Peppa did see changes, one persistent thought wouldn't go away. She missed Virginia, who'd vanished the day Peppa started on the pills. Then she got the idea to imagine that it was Virginia talking to her when Dr. Welsh spouted his truisms. *Thoughts won't kill you* and *Understanding the past will help you manage the present* were his favorites. Not nearly as eloquent as Virginia, but the method did help.

Peppa had just woken from a nap in the cushy recliner Ivan and GoGo had had delivered to the facility shortly after she arrived. The fabric, with enormous yellow flowers on a white background, perfectly matched the yellow stripe. How could they know that yellow was the only color, other than white, in her room? She imagined Ivan skimming through books on color theory, attempting to figure out which would be the most soothing for a woman who'd had a complete mental collapse while pregnant. The thought of him doing this research and making notes and then selecting the yellow and white fabric made Peppa miss her friends. Dr. Welsh said she was now ready for visitors.

Someone knocked twice, waited a few seconds, then swung open the door. GoGo appeared first, dressed in nothing special at all, almost drab. Ivan followed, sporting a snazzy bomber jacket, slim jeans, and suede loafers. Apparently a complete fashion role reversal had occurred in her absence. She held on to the arms of the recliner and hoisted her very pregnant body to a standing position. They stood in the middle of the room and did a three-way hug. GoGo was the first to cry. Then their collective sobs became so loud a nurse poked her head in.

"Everything okay?" she asked.

"Never better," Peppa said softly.

The nurse placed a box of tissues on the bed and backed out of the room. They all grabbed and blew. Peppa eased herself back into the recliner while Ivan and GoGo sat close to her on the bed.

"I love the recliner," she said. "Thank you. I mean . . . well . . . thank you."

Ivan leaned forward and took her hand. "Our dear, dear Peppa."

"No, I'm fine. Really. Really, I *am*."

"Have I made you uncomfortable?" Ivan asked.

"It's just . . . You're my first visitors, so everything's strange. And I feel embarrassed. All the trouble I've caused."

"Oh posh, Peppa," GoGo said, brushing away the awkwardness. "We've been quite bewildered. We wander around the apartment. We miss you!"

Ivan nodded.

"You were under a strain, that was obvious," GoGo continued. "But not so terrible as to cause this frightful collapse. And of course we've wondered endlessly what we could have done to prevent it."

Ivan nodded again.

"And getting information about how you were doing? That doctor of yours has been giving us bare bones. 'Peppa's *improving*.' Improving from what? We've not been informed of even a vague diagnosis. 'She's getting *stronger*.' Stronger than whom? And how strong do you need to *be* in order to get out of this place? In short, we're desperate for details."

"All true," Ivan said.

How very much the same they were. And hearing one of GoGo's rants almost made Peppa feel as if her months away had evaporated.

"So c'mon, Peppa. Spill it," Ivan prodded.

"I guess I should start with my mom," she said. "Did Dr. Welsh say anything about her?"

"*Nada. Rien. Nichts*," GoGo huffed.

"Okay. She has a mental illness."

"You told me that, Peppa," Ivan said.

"I did?"

"At The Shell. It was the day we met GoGo. Remember?"

"Oh, right. I completely forgot. Well, see, I have it too."

"Wait. What are you saying?" Ivan asked.

"I have a . . . *mental illness*."

Ivan and GoGo looked at each other, then back at her.

"I hear things," she continued.

"Like, voices?" GoGo asked. "Like, loitering on street corners, talking to invisible people?"

"No, nothing like that. It's just one voice. She gives me advice. And she's a good person. Well, she's not a *real* person. It just felt that way. It's hard to explain. But I think I was functioning pretty well."

"Of course you were," Ivan said. "I would never have guessed that you were suffering like this."

"That's the thing. I wasn't suffering. Not from her, anyway. And I'm on some drugs now that suppress her. But that was just one of my problems. Dr. Welsh says I have a cluster of disorders. It's why I've been here for so long. And don't be hard on him. I haven't wanted visitors until recently, and he needed to agree that I was ready, so it took some time."

"That makes complete sense," Ivan said.

"But did you really not know something was wrong?" she asked. "Be honest."

"I suppose looking back, there were clues." Ivan hesitated. "Okay, sometimes I'd be talking and you'd stare past me like you were watching some drama going on behind me. I just thought it was the way you concentrated. But there was something that GoGo and I both noticed. You seem to think you're overweight. And that you're unattractive."

"We didn't understand it at all," GoGo said. "*You're* not fat. *I'm* fat. And your face is exotic. A cross between Liv Ullmann and Rita Hayworth."

Ivan sighed. "Can we just agree that she's beautiful?"

"We can, and she is. But she does have Rita's eyes and Liv's lips. Which puts her into the category of *gorgeous*."

Peppa tried very hard not to flinch at that particular word. "Dr. Welsh says I have a form of body dysmorphic disorder. Usually, people obsess about one specific flaw. But I see my entire body in a way that's supposedly not real. I'm still not completely convinced, but working on it has been pretty interesting. He started off by making me look in the mirror and describe my face. And I'd say, *yeah, awful*. Then he'd tell me why it wasn't true. We did this for a while, and I found the whole exercise ridiculous. So he devised a different way. I was forbidden to look in a mirror. They even removed the one in my bathroom. Then he took a few photos of my face and we'd spend time looking at them. But only *he* was allowed to describe my features. This went on for quite a while, and I kept telling him how pointless this was too. Because I knew the truth, and how dare he, and who did he think he *was*. All that resistance stuff. But then I started to disassociate the idea of myself from the person in the photo. When he finally allowed me to look in the mirror, I honestly couldn't call myself ugly anymore."

"That's fascinating," Ivan said.

"Isn't it? I still avoid mirrors, though. I don't want to chance slipping back."

"Okay, so you fixed the face problem. What about being fat?" GoGo asked. "I've never seen you in anything other than a pup tent, but I'd stake my life that you're a perfect size seven."

"Seeing as I'm fatter than ever, there's no point thinking about it, at least until the baby gets born. Just a few weeks now." Peppa placed her hands on top of her belly and rubbed the taut skin.

"Everything seems so hopeful, Peppa," Ivan said.

She thought about the yellow stripe and the recliner and the sun and taxicabs and the nice people at the facility. All hopeful things. And she didn't want to dispel Ivan's hope, but Dr. Welsh would be very pleased with her if she was honest and did just that. "Not exactly. There was another problem. Something happened the day I went missing. It pretty much triggered my breakdown. I can't talk about it. At least not now."

The truth was, she couldn't tell them even if she wanted to. Peppa remembered being in her parents' office. And the ledger. And the red numbers. And the plumber's name. And the betrayal. But nothing immediately after, or in the subsequent six days she'd been missing. Dr. Welsh said this was her mind's way of protecting her from further trauma. In fact, it was possible she might never remember, and that was probably a good thing. He did tell her that she was found in a library, with no shoes on and one front tooth missing. She had begged the librarian to find a quote by the poet Frank O'Hara. Oddly, Peppa couldn't remember ever having read O'Hara. But the tooth had since been replaced, and Peppa insisted that the gap not be closed. She didn't want perfect front teeth reminding her of how sick she'd been.

And now she needed to shift the attention away from herself. "Tell me what happened on your end? When I didn't show up for work."

"God. I must have called you dozens of times that day," Ivan said. "It was so unlike you to not answer. We truly didn't know what to think. Then we got a call the next day from your dad. It was very early, maybe 6 a.m., and he was crying. I could barely understand him. But before he hung up, he said you were *alive*. So, you can imagine where our thoughts went. Were you hit by a bus? Assaulted? Then about an hour later, your mom called. She was coherent, very businesslike."

"That makes sense. She's completely nuts but has a steel rod for a backbone."

"She wouldn't tell us anything specific, just that you were in a facility and being taken care of. And that was reassuring, but we still didn't know why. I tried to get it out of her and was getting nowhere when all of a sudden, she gave up Welsh's direct line. He got back to me immediately. Nice man."

"He's a saint," Peppa said.

"The world could do with more like him. But hey, it's noon and I'm hungry and I know GoGo is too. We brought lunch."

Ivan grabbed a large basket they'd left by the door. GoGo laid out white china plates on a low table by her bed, along with bright orange napkins rolled into silver rings. Champagne glasses were filled, and Peppa took a sip.

"Lemonade! Perfect," she said.

"Any meal from Dean & DeLuca is worth squeezing lemons for," GoGo declared, while seasoning the sandwiches with dribbles of pesto vinaigrette.

After a few bites, Peppa was reminded of how much she missed good food. "This is so, so, so delicious!"

"What do they have you eating?" Ivan asked.

"It's all either beige or brown. I stopped guessing."

"Then I'm glad we thought to bring lunch. We've been planning the meal since Welsh green-lit us for the visit. I made crème brûlée for dessert. And speaking of food, we have some news. Tell her, GoGo."

"I'm opening a restaurant!"

"What? How?" Peppa asked.

"It's all thanks to Prince Ivan. He wrangled money out of those gazillionaires lurking about his office. They've pledged full backing for three years. And without any guarantee of a profit, if you can imagine. He must have drugged them to agree to that part. But I'll admit that Eric supervising didn't hurt. Rich people always want to hobnob with a star chef. We found a place at the northern edge of Chelsea. The kitchen needs minimal update, which means that most of the money can be used for a complete front-of-house renovation. It's all in my mind, down to the burnished copper nailheads on the upholstered wingback chairs I envision at the head of each table."

"Wow . . . so fast," Peppa said.

"One thing led to the next and we had to jump or lose it. It was pure luck," Ivan said. "But tell her the rest."

"There's *more*?" she asked.

"Ivan is going to leave LBS and start his own business. He'll work out of the apartment."

"Oh. It all sounds . . . so nice." They'd gone on without her, living their lives. Opening a restaurant. Imagining the decoration. Making career changes. Nothing had stopped them, not even her breakdown. They *were* so lucky. Now Peppa noticed a fat beetle on the wall above their heads. It struggled to climb over a thick white paint drip that had breached the yellow stripe. In all the time she'd sat in this room, she had never noticed this obvious flaw. And now she imagined the beetle was inside her head, taunting her: *They don't need you.* Virginia would never talk like this, but the drugs had taken her away. And oh, how she missed her. Peppa squeezed her eyes shut.

"Peppa, what are you doing?" Ivan said, grabbing her hand. "GoGo, get the nurse—"

"No. Nothing's wrong," Peppa said. "It's just . . . will LBS assign me to someone new? Or am I fired?"

"What? Neither. You'll be working with me, you dummy. You think I can do my job without you? Or that I'd ever want to? But no more clients. We're going to do the philanthropic work only. My lawyer is in the process of setting everything up. We've been dying to tell you. Well? What do you think?"

"But how? The baby's coming soon," she said.

"You'll live with us, just like we planned before. Tell her, GoGo."

"We already broke through to make a nursery that's connected to your bedroom. A suite of sorts. This way you'll be able to hear every whimper from the wee one. We debloated and decluttered the entire space. Ivan insisted on painting the walls white. I fought him at first, but he's right, it's the correct color. Zero reference to anything. A new start."

"And we're getting you a nanny," Ivan said. "For as long as you need. God knows *we* wouldn't know what to do with a small human. So. It's decided. No?"

"To be honest, I haven't gotten my head around leaving here yet. Except that returning to Sandy Point is out of the question. I thought I'd ask Lorraine if her second bedroom might still be available—"

"With a baby? Absolutely not. Peppa, listen to me. Starting up the new business is going to take months. There'll be plenty of time to get settled. We'll figure it out as we go. So, say yes?"

She assented with a timid smile. And with that, Ivan cracked into the crème brûlée crust, and they devoured dessert. Peppa hadn't eaten so much food at one sitting in a long time, and her stomach seemed to be crowding the baby, so she flattened the recliner and lay back. Then, the baby kicked. "You guys! Come feel."

Four hands covered her belly. They all held still, waiting for another movement.

"This always happens," Peppa said. "As soon as she moves and I say something, she stops."

"So it's a girl! And what's that I'm feeling now? Her foot?" Ivan asked.

"Who knows? She spins around all the time."

"What will you call her?" GoGo asked.

"It's bad luck to say. That's what the nurses tell me, anyway."

"Oh, what a deeply silly wives' tale. She's due soon and I need to get everything monogrammed. I've called my man on Savile Row."

"Well, there's only one name. Katherine. After your nun, Ivan."

"Peppa. That is just the dearest thing in the world."

"I'll call her Kit."

"This is perfection," GoGo said. "With only three letters, her name will fit on all her towels, every piece of bed linen, and the onesies as you call them. Her sippy cup will be Spode china. The plate for her morning gruel will be Sèvres porcelain. And I'm ordering a custom pram from Edinburgh. Not sure about the color yet—"

"Wait a minute. I'm concerned that with her name all over the place, it'll lead to self-absorption," Ivan said.

"It's true that we don't want to create a narcissist," GoGo said. "But my plan is to ply her with the best at birth, then, when she starts to walk, we'll teach her moderation. In the end, Kit will have the manners of a well-heeled thoroughbred and empathy for others like the burros who keep the thoroughbreds company."

"Nice try, honey. But Peppa will be in charge of absolutely everything."

The afternoon drifted into early evening. While Peppa rested in the recliner, Ivan and GoGo stretched out on her bed and flipped through the several copies of *Gourmet* magazine they'd brought along. She listened to them discuss the pros and cons of various table settings in photo layouts. And poke holes in Ina Garten's foolproof brined turkey recipe. Later, she probed GoGo about the debut menu he envisioned. With Eric's insistence, he capitulated to starting simple. A selection of meat, fowl, and fish dishes as main courses. Two salad options. A different appetizer each day. And four monster desserts. Ivan brought her up to date on their pending projects and the latest details about the Toilets, which by now were well into the field-testing phase. As they jabbered on, the fact that they hadn't once asked about the plumber comforted Peppa. He was a subject she still had difficulty with, and the thought of his lies still brought her to tears more often than she liked. Also, she was to face her parents' first visit the very next morning. Dr. Welsh assured her that she was ready, though Peppa couldn't stop thinking that she'd feel more ready if she had Virginia with her. But today had been a good day, and yes, things actually were quite hopeful, as Ivan said. So when they prepared to leave, Peppa confirmed again that she and Kit would live with them. And she'd like the pram to be yellow.

The next morning, she woke very early from a troubling dream. Her parents had kidnapped her with the intention of forcing her to marry the plumber. The strange part was that she and the plumber, whom they'd also kidnapped, were tied up together, but neither wanted to be a couple anymore. When Dr. Welsh stopped by her room later, she recounted the dream and how unsettled it made her feel. So much so, that she wanted to cancel the visit. He reminded her that this kind of dream was in no way a predictor of her parents' frame of mind—just boilerplate anxiety. This sounded plausible. But his interpretation of the plumber, that being tied together meant they had experienced the emotional attachment of a bonded couple, was some major Jungian BS. The plumber was a confirmed fraud and a liar. And now just thinking of it sent a shudder through her body. Peppa hoped it was Virginia trying her best to break through the barrier of pills to say something along the lines of, **I shan't pay attention to dreams or their supposed interpretations.** Yes, if Virginia were able, that's exactly the type of thing she'd say.

The knock came. She waited. Then, a weaker attempt. She half whispered, "Come in," hoping they wouldn't hear and just go away. But her mom opened the door, looking almost too poised. Her dad shuffled in after, haggard and too thin. Dr. Welsh pulled up chairs to surround her, and suddenly she felt slightly haughty, like a queen deigning to receive her subjects. Peppa clasped her hands under her enormous belly as if to emphasize that a new life had grown without any help from them, and that she and her baby were just fine, thank you. But before a word was spoken by anyone, her dad started to cry. Peppa looked at Dr. Welsh, gesturing to him with her eyes as if to say, *Do something . . . stop him.*

"Come on now, Declan. Let's not start off on a rocky path," her mom said with irritation.

He snuffed and sat up straight. "It's just seeing her. And that's our grandbaby." He pointed to the general area below Peppa's head. "But yeah, I'll be okay."

"Mr. and Mrs. Ryan, Peppa knows that you and I have not had any conversations with regard to her condition, how she's doing, or any aspect of her treatment. I know how difficult it was for you when I explained the ethics of confidentiality, and up until now Peppa has not wanted contact. That said, I encouraged her to agree to this meeting because obviously the baby will be born very soon. Peppa will have much to deal with, and I didn't want this opportunity for a conversation within a safe environment to be passed by. You should also know that today, my advocacy continues to be on behalf of Peppa alone. Her emotional health must be primary, and I will not allow the progress we've made to be jeopardized. In fact, this objective should be at the top of our collective intention. Can I get agreement on that from you both?"

They nodded—her dad vigorously, her mom with grudging acceptance.

"Great, and thank you," Dr. Welsh said. "I have no hard rules for a meeting such as this, but may I suggest that you each take turns to say hello and also, very briefly, express what you hope to get out of this conversation. Does anyone want to start?"

Peppa smiled at Dr. Welsh and thought, poor guy. Here he was, grandstanding on her behalf, warning them to be good. Practically wagging his finger at them. But she knew they wouldn't behave, especially her mom. And neither of them would go first, because they were cowards.

"Mom. Dad," she said.

They'd both been staring into their laps, but now looked up, startled.

"You've lost weight, Dad," Peppa said. "Please make sure you're eating enough. And Mom, you look the best I've seen in a long time."

They sank further into their chairs, seemingly chagrined by her gracious introduction.

"Anyway," she went on, "thanks for making the trip, but you should know that I only agreed to this meeting because Dr. Welsh thought it was important, and I value his opinion. There's not much I want to say other than I understand a lot of what happened to me and why. But I don't need for you to understand any of that. So, there you have it. I'm doing fine, and you don't have to worry because—"

"*Daughter*," her mom blurted out. "A mother doesn't stop worrying just because the kid says to. When you have your child, you'll understand."

By some miracle, Peppa held herself back from reacting.

"And if you won't tell us anything," her mom continued, "what's the point of the meeting?"

"Exactly," Peppa said. "There is no point. And you're free to leave."

"Oh no, young lady. Don't you dare start with your tricks—"

"Please, Mrs. Ryan," Dr. Welsh broke in. "Let's structure this another way. Why don't you tell Peppa what *you've* experienced? Can you contribute that?"

"Contribute?" Patrice said. "What a curious word choice. We've contributed everything she's ever needed. Given her the best home life we knew how. There's nothing the child's wanted for."

"I meant contribute to this meeting." Dr. Welsh paused and took a deep breath. "Mrs. Ryan, you understand that Peppa had a complete mental breakdown. Right?"

"I suppose so."

"So, given this, you must have feelings about it. Concerns. Can you at least assure your daughter that you've been worried about her?"

She whacked the idea away with her entire arm. "She already knows that."

Now Peppa had to keep herself from smiling, because her mom was showing Dr. Welsh precisely who she was, something Peppa had been struggling for months to describe accurately and with not much success.

"Don't you think this might be an opportunity to remind her?" Dr. Welsh asked with rare exasperation.

"Absolutely not. And it's ridiculous that you think it necessary. I'm her mother. She knows very well what I feel for her. A child understands these things. The words remain unspoken for good reason. The child must learn to be self-sufficient. Coddling does them no good. That's the way her father and I were raised. The child too. And I have no regrets about it if that's what you're going to try and drag out of me."

Clouds had collected outside and suddenly the room turned glum, so Peppa turned on the lamp sitting next to the recliner. Its light cast a particularly harsh glow on her mom's face as she furiously dug into her purse, trying to find something more meaningful than Dr. Welsh to focus on. Her dad was crying again.

"For God's sake, Declan, stop," Patrice said. "Pull yourself together and we'll go."

"Are you sure you want to leave, Mrs. Ryan?" Dr. Welsh asked. "Think about this. We can discuss your reticence."

"Reticence. Now we're on to the *fancy* words. All you need to know is that the child and I are cut from the same cloth. We often have the same viewpoint. So, like she said before, there is no point to this meeting. You should listen to her more closely, Doctor."

They were out the door, and Peppa turned to Dr. Welsh with a sympathetic smile.

"I'm really sorry," she said.

"No, Peppa. I don't need protecting. *You* do. From a therapeutic standpoint, she's fascinating. But my heart goes out to you—what you've had to live with."

"It's so strange the way she talked about me, like I was some example of her child-rearing theories."

"I imagine she has to do it this way—to separate herself from you. Seeing you as a person who's had her own trauma is clearly not possible for your mother. Too dangerous."

Dr. Welsh began to close up the messy binder he used to take notes, though in this case there had been none to take, when the door opened and Peppa's dad reappeared. Peppa looked around the room, thinking maybe they'd forgotten something.

"I've sent your mother home in a cab," he said. "Peppa, there are things we need to talk about."

"Dad, please. I'm done."

He collapsed into a chair and wiped his eyes. "Brendon wants to see you."

"And I don't want to hear this."

"He's the father."

"So what?" she said.

"But we don't understand."

"You heard what Mom said. She doesn't want to understand."

"Not her. I mean me and Brendon."

"No. I won't do this. It's . . . it's a very bad subject. *Very* bad."

"What are you talking about?"

"C'mon, Dad. The *money*."

"What about it? I know you saw the checks."

"Exactly."

"Okay. The drugs seem to be working."

Peppa looked at Dr. Welsh for a reaction, but his face remained flat. He was good at that.

"Whose drugs? Mom's?" Peppa asked.

"No. Brendon's sister."

Her dad's eyes blinked with bewilderment and his hands shook badly. Just like when, as a much younger person, she'd sit in his lap and they'd cry because there was nothing either of them could do to help the woman they were trying to save and love. Peppa wanted to grab hold of his hands, to stop the shaking and the blinking and the entire memory. But then, the baby started to kick. No. It wasn't Kit. More like a strong pop that caused her to scramble out of the recliner and walk to the very center of the room. And when her water broke, releasing warm gushes down her legs and into her shoes, Dr. Welsh and her dad, and then Peppa herself, started to laugh.

TEN SHADES OF YELLOW

PEPPA YAWNED AND FLUTTERED HER FINGERS OVER THE CAESAREAN SCAR, pressing down to see if it hurt. Not much pain anymore, only itchy now. GoGo had left a glass of water and Tylenol on her nightstand, just in case. But she'd mostly avoided taking painkillers of any sort since Kit's birth the previous month. In fact, Peppa had begged Dr. Welsh to let her stop the drugs that kept Virginia quiet. She didn't want anything to seep into her milk and harm her daughter. He balked at first, but they reached a compromise. Peppa would suspend the drugs and nurse for now, then switch to formula and resume them once Kit had received sufficient nutrients from her milk.

At 4 a.m., a low moon shot light across Peppa's bedroom. She took several gulps of water, tiptoed to the bathroom, then dropped onto the toilet. Through the closed door to the nursery, she could hear Nanny singing to Kit. GoGo had been teaching the woman something other than "Mary Had a Little Lamb," and this one was an old Scottish ditty, filled with words like *hath* and *dost*. Kit squawked and Peppa's hands jumped to her breasts. She made her way to the nursery and sat in the rocker. Nanny nestled Kit into Peppa's arms, and the girl immediately found her favorite breast. After ten minutes, Peppa deftly switched. The next thing she knew, Ivan was jostling her shoulder, a cup of tea and a warm blueberry scone within arm's reach.

"What time is it?" she asked, kissing Kit's head.

"Just after seven."

"Wow, that was a long sleep. She'll be on me again soon. Let me scarf something down." Peppa handed Kit to Ivan, then slurped some tea and bit into the scone.

"How's the incision?" he asked.

"Good. Should we take her outside today?"

"The doctor said as long as you can lift a gallon of milk without pain, you're cleared. And perfectly fine for Kit."

"Should Nanny come with us?"

"Nah. Just us four. Cozier."

"GoGo still asleep?" she asked.

"He just woke up. Listen, I want to run something by you. Why don't you come with me tomorrow morning? I pretty much cleared out my office last week, but I'll be making formal goodbyes. I suspect LBS has a send-off brewing, and I know everyone would love to see you. And the baby."

"And GoGo too."

Ivan nodded. "Yes, of course. Might as well be fully out. Anyway, who was I kidding? Except *you*."

Peppa laughed. "Just call me the hick from backwoods Queens."

"I'll get a town car to shuttle us. And if you want, we could eat lunch at Windows on the World."

"Fancy! It's strange, but I feel quite different today. Like I can actually do stuff. See people. Go to a restaurant. It wasn't like that yesterday."

"So it's a plan?"

"Absolutely. I'll sit in a corner and let everyone come to me," she said with a giggle.

"Queen Peppa. Princess Kit."

"King Ivan."

"Make that King *GoGo*. In case you hadn't noticed, he's pretty much Lord of the Realm around here," Ivan said, rolling his eyes.

"But we love it, right?"

"Who wouldn't love that butterball?"

Kit was by now waking up and started to fuss, so Peppa pulled one shoulder of her nightgown down, and Ivan transferred the baby.

"You want a proper breakfast after this feeding?" he asked.

"I'm famished."

"Okay, I'll get GoGo on that. Then we'll go for the walk."

While Kit nursed, Peppa looked around the room. Pretty blue and white dotted Swiss cotton tie-back curtains. Custom furniture GoGo had painted in ten shades of yellow, an homage to what was now Peppa's favorite color. She dug her toes into the thick pile carpet. Peppa had never known what it felt like to be pampered in this way. But it was more than that. Something close to devotion. Throughout the two weeks in the hospital, while preemie Kit resolved a stubborn case of jaundice in the NICU and Peppa battled the infection she'd contracted after her C-section, Ivan and GoGo played guardian angels. She'd been unaware of them for much of the time due to a high fever, but the nurses later told her that they'd held and fed Kit every day. Then, once Peppa crossed the threshold to the apartment, GoGo crowned himself master of all things Kit. Each evening, he selected the color of her onesie for the following day with booties to match. Twice daily, he made sure to fluff and refold the blankets in her bassinet for something called the *cloud effect* he insisted was important for infants. She and Ivan indulged him. But when he custom-ordered a miniature gold box from Tiffany encrusted with rose-cut diamonds, for Kit's first nail clippings, Peppa said the idea was ridiculous and the expense preposterous. But GoGo explained that it was an important tradition, citing Mary, Queen of Scots as source material, and who was Peppa to challenge the royals? So when the treasure took pride of place on Kit's chest of drawers, Ivan then decried that all indulgences for the girl had been fully satisfied.

Peppa thought, *Dear Virginia, if you're there, why am I so lucky?*

When she entered the kitchen, Peppa found GoGo attacking something on the stove with a whisk in one hand and a spatula in the other.

"Peppa," he said. "You look stunning in that vintage DVF number I found on eBay. The jersey fabric still puddles beautifully."

"I just wear what you hand me in the morning. I have zero style."

"You don't need any. I have more than enough for the entire building. But sit. I'm making omelets with brie from Belgium. Potatoes planted by 1960s ex-revolutionaries living in rural Pennsylvania. Fresh bread from that place in the Bronx, the name eludes me. Butter churned at some farm where the cows are treated like first cousins. Sadly, the eggs I cannot vouch for." He set a plate in front of her. "I'm testing this for the restaurant, and I need your honest opinion. So don't stuff multiple foods into your mouth at the same time."

"Is that what I do?"

"I'm sorry to say that I've observed this unfortunate behavior from time to time."

"I'll do my very best," she said, plucking a single home fry from the plate and depositing it into her mouth with fanfare.

Ivan came in and GoGo began singing a song in his uppermost falsetto involving needing and wanting, followed by more wanting and needing. Then, a sloppy and prolonged kiss as proof.

"You guys!" Peppa wailed. "Keep that stuff in the bedroom. There's a minor child afoot now."

"She needs to learn about love *somehow*," GoGo huffed. "And what better way than from one of the most beautiful lyrics ever written?"

"It is lovely. Who wrote it?" Peppa asked.

"Jimmy Webb. 'Wichita Lineman.' 1968. Capitol Records. Glen Campbell. He used to headline for me," GoGo said.

"Glen's playing Sioux Falls next month," Ivan said. "GoGo wants us all to go."

"We could rent a supercharged camper and loop around a few states," GoGo said. "Peppa's never been *anywhere*."

"Thanks a lot, GoGo."

"Well, it happens to be true."

"Honey, it sounds . . . compelling," Ivan said, "but I'm not sure this is the time for a road trip. You *are* opening a restaurant, and I *am* starting a business. And with an infant? Let's put a pin in it for now."

"I never get my way," GoGo sighed.

"Right," Ivan said. "Anyway, Peppa. Your dad just called."

She stopped chewing midmotion.

"He wants to drive in today and see you and the baby."

"I can't. No."

"Now just hold on there," Ivan said with rare impatience.

"Ohhhh boy," she said, pushing her meal to the center of the table.

"You don't like it at all?" GoGo asked.

"I love it," she said, "but your boyfriend is about to yell at me."

Ivan leaned across the table. "Have I ever yelled at you? Even a hint?"

"I guess not," she said, turning to take in the north view. The church spires were sharply etched against the bluest sky she'd ever seen. But no clouds. And still, no Virginia.

"Look at me," Ivan said.

She snapped her head back.

"Have I *ever* lied to you?" he asked.

"Not that I remember."

"And do you believe I want the best for you?"

"I'm not sure I can do it today," she whined, feeling tears well up.

"Do you believe . . . I want . . . the best . . . for you," he repeated slowly.

Peppa wiped her eyes and sighed. "Yes."

"Good. We can meet him in Gramercy Park. I have the key from a client."

"But what did he say?"

"Nothing much. Just that he'd meet us anywhere."

"Ivan, I'm still settling in. Things have been cheerful. I'm afraid of . . . slipping, I guess you'd call it. And I'm still suspicious of what my dad said that day when my water broke. He and my mom have always been squirrely with the truth when it suits them."

"You mean about the sister," Ivan said.

"Yes. And the money. Dr. Welsh had a brief session with them while I was recovering in the hospital. They described our family in a way he knew wasn't true because he'd already gotten the complete background from me. Basically sanitizing everything. Even my mom's many disappearances, denying that any of it ever happened. And they refused to talk about Brendon, saying it was a private family matter." Peppa paused for effect. "Ivan, he warned me to *be very careful*. Exactly those words."

"Well, just now on the phone your dad sounded pretty desperate."

"Peppa, darling. You know how I detest even the *idea* of a desperate person," GoGo said while finishing her omelet. "But we'd be there with you."

"And it might not go as badly as you think," Ivan added.

Their optimism was getting to her. Why couldn't they take Dr. Welsh's warning to heart as she did? "At least agree with me that he's highly unreliable."

"You'll get no argument from me about that," Ivan said.

"And only my dad, right? Not my mom."

"He didn't say. But I can make that clear if that's what you need."

"I can't do both of them. What time did he say?"

"Whenever," Ivan said.

"I have to shower."

"So do we. How about I tell him noon at the southeast corner of the park. If we leave here about 11:15, we could walk it."

"That sounds good," she said. "I haven't moved my body in forever."

"Okay, I'll set it up," Ivan said while walking out.

"Not my mother!" she yelled through the door.

"I know!"

After fussing about what and what not to bring on Kit's first walk, GoGo stuffed everything possible into the pram: enough diapers for a week, lavender-scented wipes, and multiple pacifiers. They proceeded like a sleepy processional, taking turns adjusting the sun guard whenever a corner was turned. Ivan and GoGo tag-teamed peeking into the pram every few minutes to make sure she was still properly swaddled. All the usual behavior associated with people who had no idea what they were doing with an infant, and Peppa certainly saw herself in this category. One woman sidled up to give unsolicited advice. Walk faster, she advised. The baby will get used to it, she assured them. Peppa appreciated the suggestion. GoGo found it an affront. Ivan remained neutral. And on they crawled.

Finally, they approached the western edge of Gramercy Park. After unlocking the gate, Ivan steered them to a bench that faced a particularly fancy brownstone.

"There he is," Peppa said, pointing to a white truck idling at the far side of the park. "I should nurse her first. But I don't want my dad to see."

"We'll go over and occupy him. How much time do you need?" Ivan asked.

Peppa leaned into the pram. Kit was just waking up. "Give me fifteen minutes."

Though the temperature had already reached the mid-eighties, an enormous elm kept the sun's heat at bay. Peppa sat on the shaded bench and pulled a towel from the very bottom of the pram. Once Kit settled on her breast, she draped the towel across the whole operation for privacy and watched as Ivan and GoGo approached the truck. It was parked in an area where trees didn't obscure her view, and the sun seemed to act as a spotlight. Peppa immediately became engrossed in a theater of pantomime.

Her dad climbed out of the truck, and they ushered him into the park. Ivan talked for a while, gesturing with his hands, the motions gentle, placating. Her dad seemed to listen intently, nodding every ten seconds or so. Now Ivan pointed to her, and she quickly averted her gaze, not wanting to make eye contact. When she looked back, her dad was performing his part. He looked to be pleading with Ivan. She now imagined that Ivan had told him he would need to wait for her to finish nursing his grandchild before they'd allow him to talk to her. And she could hardly blame him for being frustrated. But as the scene played out further, Peppa realized it wasn't that at all. Now her dad was sitting on the bench, head down, chin against his sternum. He spoke for several uninterrupted minutes, which was a long time for a man of succinct words. Throughout, his posture seemed to collapse even more, as if yielding to minor blows. Ivan and GoGo didn't move an inch.

Suddenly, GoGo took a few quick steps back. But Ivan moved closer and placed his hand on her dad's shoulder. He stood, staggered to the iron fence, and grabbed on. Ivan supported his elbow to keep him from falling. Now they all sat on the bench, her dad in the middle. GoGo and Ivan talked to him from either side, with what looked to be an effort to convince him of something important, and Peppa couldn't imagine what. All the while, her dad stared straight ahead, not reacting to their words. Finally, Ivan looked over to Peppa and nodded. She settled Kit in the pram and made her way across the park.

"Daddy?"

He jerked his head up like he'd been slapped. His clothes were filthy, his beard ragged, like an insane razor had made a crisscross of stripes on his cheeks. He took in a quick breath at the sight of her, then let it out slowly. Peppa smelled alcohol.

"What's happened?" she said.

"Oh, Peppa," he groaned.

"Not good news," Ivan said.

"Tell me. Tell me now, Dad."

"Your mother's not well," Declan said.

"She's off her pills again?"

"No. Not like that."

"For God's sake, *what*?"

Her dad pulled a flask out of his pocket and took several swallows, then looked at Ivan.

Ivan hesitated. "It's . . . pancreatic cancer."

Peppa shook her head. "No. How? How can that be? She's always been strong. Barely a flu."

"You know your mother," Declan said. "She ignores everything."

"Oh Jesus, Daddy. But there's treatment."

He said nothing.

"*Right*?" she pressed.

He took another swig.

"Why are you drinking in the middle of the day?"

"The doctor called this morning."

"On a Sunday?"

"We'd been waiting on him. More test results. But that's only part of why I needed to see you. That day we saw you at the facility? We found out about her disease just that morning. So your mother wasn't at her best. I wanted you to know that."

Peppa lifted Kit from the pram and presented her. "Kit, meet your grandaddy."

He waved her off. "Not now. I'm on the sharp edge of a drunk."

"It'll be okay."

"Maybe for a wee bit."

She placed Kit, now asleep, against his chest. He smiled weakly and rubbed her cheek with his palm.

"No," he said suddenly. "Take her back."

"Are you sure?" Peppa asked.

"I'm not fit."

Peppa handed Kit to Ivan and sat next to her dad. "You have to tell me more about Mom. She'll have treatment of some sort. Right?"

He looked at Ivan again. "Can you tell her?"

"No, *you* tell me, Daddy," she pleaded.

"Peppa, while you were sitting across the park, I explained everything to these two. They're good men. They'll tell you. I've no strength for it now."

Peppa knelt in front of her father and looked into his eyes. "Daddy, I'm so sorry. I'll help you. Whatever she needs."

"Look, I need to go. I don't feel good leaving Patrice for too long."

Peppa ushered him to his truck. He turned the ignition and rolled down the window.

"Drive slow, Dad. It's all you need to get stopped."

He started to pull away but braked and stuck his head out the window. "I got Brendon a job with the city. It's union. He needs to hear from you. Think about it, Peppa."

She watched him drive off, signaling right but taking a left turn. Ivan had come up behind her and pulled on her arm. "Let's go home."

"What didn't he tell me?"

"It's metastasized everywhere. She's got maybe a month. Your dad's putting her into hospice sometime this week."

The walk home had been grim, like a death march. And now back at the apartment while Nanny attended to Kit in the nursery, they sat on the sofa, a pod of three with Peppa in the middle. She'd rarely seen the Hudson this rough. Whitecaps popped up through the black water. Tugs labored. Sailboats pressed forward, a futile effort.

"When's your next session with Dr. Welsh?" Ivan asked.

"End of next week. Why?"

"GoGo and I think you should schedule one sooner."

Peppa frowned. "I'll think about it."

"Remember your discharge meeting with Welsh? The three of us?"

"What's your point?"

"If GoGo and I felt you needed Welsh, you promised you'd do it."

"I'm pretty sure I'll be okay until next week. Anyway, I want to process things on my own."

"A noble thought, but that's not what you agreed to."

"I'd like to try." Now the sailboats looked to be fighting not only the wind but also the tide change. *They're doomed*, Peppa thought. And still, no Virginia.

Ivan moved to one end of the sofa and turned to address her directly. "You were recently released from the facility. You've had a caesarean and contracted a serious infection. You're sleep-deprived with a newborn. Your mom is close to death. With all of that, do you really think you should wait a week to see Welsh?"

Peppa didn't know a damned thing. Only that Ivan had rolled out all the terrible facts of her life like a dirty red carpet and, in truth, she didn't want to face any of it. "Let me do it my way. Just this once. Please?"

"Sorry, but no."

"Peppa, try to see reason," GoGo said.

"I can't," she croaked. "I just need the day to cry. I know I'll feel better tomorrow."

"Crying for an entire day is not a solution," Ivan said. "And do I need to remind you that you're off the pills?"

"I'm going back on in just a few weeks. What can possibly happen?"

"I admire your optimism, but no deal."

Peppa squirmed. She'd never seen Ivan act like such a bulldog.

"I'm getting very bored with this thread," he pressed. "And your resistance is telling."

"Shit. I'll call him tomorrow," she said. "After we get back from the office party."

Hoping the entire subject would be dropped, Peppa forced a smile. But Ivan still looked like he wanted to throw her overboard.

"What now?" she asked.

"Brendon."

"Oh, God. No."

"You need to call him."

"Come *on*. It's *my* life," she whimpered.

"Actually, that's only partially true. There are people involved, not the least of whom is Kit. Brendon's daughter."

"But I told you how even Dr. Welsh wasn't sure what the truth was. So how can I trust him?"

"True, there's still ambiguity. And yes, your parents are not exactly trustworthy. But you shouldn't just transfer all that onto Brendon. I'm sure he's got a story of his own."

"Peppa, all we're suggesting is that you give the plumber a chance to explain," GoGo reasoned.

GoGo being *reasonable*. And the sailboats—not turning around. And the people sailing them—complete amateurs. They should have taken courses. They should have studied the tides. They probably didn't know the first thing about clouds. And was *this* the way life was going to be? Both of them ganging up on her? *Dear Virginia, where the hell are you?*

Ivan pressed. "Remember that day at the restaurant?"

Peppa sighed. "Vaguely."

"You promised us then that you'd discuss things with Brendon *that night*. Remember? GoGo, back me up."

"Indeed. Le Bernardin. Scallops. The pumpkin mousse—"

"I *remember*," she said.

"You still need to keep that promise." Ivan pointed to her phone lying on the coffee table. "So pick that thing up and punch in a bunch of numbers. Come on, GoGo. Let's leave her to it."

Ivan hugged her hard, and GoGo triple-kissed her on the cheeks. They went to the kitchen and left the door open as they began to assemble guacamole. Ivan commented that it was much too spicy, but GoGo liked the bite. They bickered about it for a while and then decided to make an entirely fresh batch. That meant going to the specialty grocer around the corner to purchase half a dozen perfectly ripe avocados. And Peppa knew this was probably meant to give her the privacy to make good on her promise. She looked back toward the Hudson. The sailboats had finally given up and turned around, succumbing to the power of the river. In fact, they had no choice but to do so. And Peppa thought, there never *were* any choices in life, not really. She pulled her phone off the coffee table.

"Peppa? Is it you?" Brendon answered.

"Yes. It's me."

"My *God*."

"I know," she said.

"I tried to reach you."

"They took my phone away."

"Are you okay?" he asked.

"I'm better now."

"I have so many questions."

"I know."

"How is she?"

"Beautiful. An angel."

"Healthy?"

"Oh yes."

"What do you want to do?" he asked. "I mean, about me."

"I think you should see her."

"And *you*."

"Yes, me too."

"I can be there in an hour."

"No. Not today," she said.

"When?"

"Tomorrow morning?"

"Yes, but I have a job," he said. "Downtown at the Twin Towers."

"Is seven too early?"

"It's fine. But what about you?"

"I'm up all day and all night. It doesn't matter."

"Okay then."

"Brendon."

"Yes."

"What are you reading?"

"Virginia. *To the Lighthouse.*"

A CRISP AND CLEAR MORNING

SHE WAS DREAMING ABOUT HER MOM, IMPROBABLY DRESSED IN A BALL GOWN with a tiara on her head and a sash across her bosom. She waved a wand in circles, sparklers flying from the tip. Dozens of people outstretched their hands, trying to touch the edge of her hem as she twirled. In the dream, her mom was a beauty queen. An adored idol. A person who'd gone all the way to the top and had the crown to prove it. In real life, this is what Peppa had always wanted for her—to twirl and twirl and twirl, just as she wished and for as long as she needed. Because somewhere inside all that madness was the brightest shining star trying her best to glow. Now something or someone pushed against Peppa's shoulder, but she wasn't ready to let go. If only her mom had taken the shock therapy that had been suggested years ago, but terrified her too much to even consider. If only the perfect drug cocktail had been arrived at so her mom wouldn't stop taking them every couple of months. If only she had agreed to talk therapy, an exercise she insisted was for people of weak character. And if only Peppa had not been so dedicated to her own outrage the day her mom had visited. Then she would have noticed what had been so obvious. That her mom's potential for twirling had ended.

And Peppa thought, *Oh Virginia, if only*.

She opened her eyes to GoGo wiggling his fingers.

"Yoo-hoo. Your plumber is here."

She turned over to look at the clock. "But it's just after six. I told him seven," she groaned.

"Apparently being ridiculously early is considered acceptable in some distant land."

"He's probably nervous. What was he to do, stand on the street corner?"

"Well, no harm. Ivan is plying him with coffee. Come on, Miss Size Seven, get thee up. I have a few outfits for you to consider."

A clothing rack had been rolled into her bedroom with three dresses hanging from the pole. Having thrown out every muumuu she owned, and whether she wanted it or not, GoGo had been assembling a new wardrobe. And to Peppa's surprise, she was gradually becoming a fashion junkie. And with opinions.

"Right off the bat, I like the floral," she said. "It suits me."

"Agreed. Stella McCartney. Go have a sponge-off."

Since Kit had been born, Peppa had become super-efficient with dispatching morning rituals. She hit the toilet, spritzed in the shower, jabbed at her teeth, and pulled on fresh underwear, all in about ten minutes. When she returned, GoGo dropped the dress over her head. Peppa struck a pose. He nodded with satisfaction.

"That'll work nicely. But tighten the belt a bit. Ruffle your hair. Pull back your shoulders. Might as well show off those milky boobs while they last. I'll trust you to pick a pair of shoes on your own, but the blue and white Blahnik kitten heels would look divine. No pressure."

Just then Ivan walked in, looking frantic. "My God, what's taking so long? I've had four espressos and I'm so buzzed I'm starting to tell him things I shouldn't. GoGo, you have to spell me."

"With pleasure. I'm dying to tell him about the one and only time I attempted sex with a woman. If memory serves, I recall a waterbed was in the room. In any case, straight men need to understand women through the eyes of a gay man. One day he'll thank me."

With GoGo off to his mission of benevolence, Peppa sat at the edge of the bed and slipped her feet into the Blahniks. Ivan was leaning against the doorjamb with his arms crossed. He wore a black suit, black bow tie, and a scorching white shirt.

"You look positively scary," she said. "That's a compliment."

"Taken. What's your plan?"

"I don't have one."

"Did you really have to ask him to come today? And so *early*."

"I know. And I'm sorry," she said. "But when I talked to him yesterday, it just seemed like the thing to do."

"Well, I've got the car set to arrive at seven-thirty. The party starts at nine."

"What's it now?"

"Seven exactly. That gives you about half an hour with him. Now, will you please get to the kitchen? God knows what GoGo is divulging."

She flew out of the bedroom and when she approached the kitchen, she could hear GoGo deep into the waterbed odyssey.

"All that *sloshing*. I believe I shouted *ahoy* at one point. Altogether a perplexing experience."

"Sounds awful," Brendon said with sympathy.

"Truly dreadful. So, what's your story, big boy?"

Peppa pushed the door open.

"Oh! Here she is," GoGo said. "Brendon, it's been a dream talking with you, but I suspect my boyfriend needs some manner of attention right about now."

Brendon had lost weight. His clothes dripped off his frame, his cheeks had hollowed out, and his eyes seemed to protrude more than ever. His fragility was palpable, and a wound-up vigilance inside of Peppa uncoiled a notch.

"Sorry. He can get weird sometimes," she said.

"Is he famous or something? He said he partied with Mick Jagger."

"Yeah, he had a big career at one time."

"You look so *different*," he said.

"I do? Oh, right. GoGo's got me all styled up."

"It's nice."

"You think?"

"Quite posh."

"I lost my waist pretty fast. I was big."

He took a deep breath but said nothing.

"Let's go see Kit," she said.

Peppa led him through the apartment and when they got to the nursery, she immediately guided him to the crib. He leaned over and quietly gasped.

"Lord. I can't believe I'm seeing her. Can I hold her?" he asked.

"Of course. Just support her head."

He rolled Kit nicely into the crook of his arm and stared for some time, kissing her forehead at intervals. "She's a beauty."

"She has the shape of your face," Peppa said. "The chin too. Do you see it?"

"No, can't say I do. But I think I see your eyes. Almonds."

"I want to show you something." She grabbed a stack of photos Ivan was in the process of sifting through for a picture album and picked out one of Kit asleep. Then she retrieved a photo of Brendon that was propped against the Tiffany nail clipping container on top of the chest.

"You have my picture," he said with surprise. "How?"

"I stole it," she admitted with a guilty smile. "There were a bunch of them at your place. You were going to send them back to Ireland. Remember? I figured you wouldn't miss it. Anyway, come sit on the sofa."

He sat next to her and laid Kit across his knees. Her arms flopped to either side. "Is this okay? I mean her position."

"Oh sure. She's still asleep, so she's comfortable." Peppa presented the two images. "You can see the similarities more easily this way."

"Yeah, I get it. The shape, for sure. Maybe my ears too? Poor dear!" They both laughed at this, because Peppa had occasionally made fun of his big ears.

"Ivan predicts her hair will turn auburn. Like yours," she said.

Just then, Kit scrunched up her face and segued to a wail within seconds.

"There she goes," Peppa said. She unbuttoned the front of her dress and pulled a breast from her nursing bra. Brendon handed their daughter over. While Kit was occupied with her meal, Peppa figured this was the time to explain things about herself and ask the questions she was afraid to hear the answers to.

"Let's not talk about any of it now," he said as if reading her mind.

"How did you know? That I don't know how to begin?"

"I just do," he said with a shrug. "Anyway, we haven't the time now. I've got to get to the subway."

He started to get up but Peppa grabbed his hand. "Wait. You said you're working at the Twin Towers?"

"Not working exactly. I'm learning about HVAC systems in tall buildings."

"You mean no more plumbing?"

"Well, I don't see myself installing toilets for the rest of my life, so I'm checking this out."

"Ivan's office is in the Towers, and we're headed there too. We have a car service coming. You could ride along with us."

"That sounds grand. But are you sure? Shouldn't you ask them first?"

"They're my friends, not my guardians. Kit's coming too."

He reached over and rubbed the soft spot at the top of Kit's head. "I'd like that."

They piled into the car. Ivan sat in the front seat next to the driver, while Peppa settled between GoGo and Brendon in the back. Kit slept against her chest in the Snugli. She heard the weather report from CBS News—temperatures in the mid-seventies with a light north breeze. A crisp and clear morning. The sports report that followed announced the Yankees' home game against the Cubs that evening. Peppa thought of her dad and how little patience he had for America's obsession with a bunch of athletes milling about for the greater part of a three-hour game. And that reminded her of the first client she'd met and how she'd challenged him about his love of baseball, and with precisely that argument. In subsequent encounters, she'd reined herself in by defaulting to the guy's health, and in this way they reached a comfort-able détente. But a couple of days before her breakdown when, as usual, she'd met that client at the elevator, he pulled her to the end of a corridor and stood much too close. Peppa was pretty sure he was drunk, so she prepared herself for either some kind of takedown or some kind of come-on. But he inflicted neither. He told Peppa that he knew he could be quite a bastard, as the women in his life sometimes called him. And that he was very sorry if he'd been a bastard to her too. She told him she didn't think he was a bastard, at least not in his heart. And if she'd ever been sassy to him, well, she was also sorry. They both started to weep, but for different reasons. On that day, Peppa was pregnant, and no one knew it. The man had been terribly mean to everyone he professed to love, and finally understood it. Many months had passed since Peppa first met that client at the elevator on the ninety-sixth floor. And weirdly, she missed him. He wasn't such a bad sort and, in fact, he was the good omen that opened the door to Peppa's entire life. Because if he'd complained about her to Ivan that first day, she would have been fired on the spot and back working for her parents. Then there might never have been a date with the plumber. And even if there had been, she was sure it would have gone differently. And then Kit wouldn't be propped against her chest at this moment, dreaming whatever it was that infants dreamt about while gumming their fists.

And Peppa thought, *Dear Virginia, did you hear all that?*

They arrived at the Towers too early to go up to the office, so Ivan instructed the driver to circle the block for a while.

"Is anybody besides me hungry?" Peppa asked after just one go-around.

Ivan turned around from the front seat. "GoGo and I managed yogurt and granola. Can you hang on? We'll be eating at the office."

"I'm kind of shaky."

At afternoon tea the other day, Vanessa introduced Leonard and myself to a peculiar pastry; a doughy affair referred to as a bagel. And now we cannot bear to face the day without one.

"*What*!?" Peppa yipped. Virginia. Of course. She was off her drugs!

"How's that, Peppa?" Ivan asked.

Bagel.

"Um . . . there's a bagel shop just a block away. Let's go."

"It'll be mobbed this time of morning and take forever," Ivan protested.

Bagel; Bagel.

"Please, Ivan? I've got to have a bagel. GoGo. Tell him we have to get the bagels."

"It *is* fashionable to be late to one's own party, darling," GoGo said.

Ivan shot him an annoyed glance. "Peppa, is this absolutely necessary?"

Bagel; Bagel; Bagel.

Wow. If Virginia felt this strongly about bagels, Peppa needed to draw her guns. "I'm a new mother. I have cravings. I'm nursing. I'm shaking from hunger. I *really* need a bagel. *Now*."

The driver slammed his fist on the steering wheel. "I take you bagel place."

While Ivan and GoGo got in line to order, Peppa and Brendon found a table toward the front with a view to the Towers across the plaza.

"Where's your job—I mean, which tower?" she asked, pointing to the buildings.

"We're starting at the top of the North Tower," Brendon said. "There's a restaurant up there, I think. I've never been in either, so I'm pretty excited."

"Yeah, I felt that way too when I started working there. Ivan's office is in the South Tower. The ninety-sixth floor. You can feel it sway when the wind's up. It's pretty cool."

Ivan and GoGo returned with two trays heaped with various bagels and spreads, a pile of scrambled eggs, perfectly charred bacon, and coffees.

"I forgot how great the food is here," Ivan said. "Good idea after all, Peppa."

"And I've never had an everything bagel," GoGo said.

"We have them in Ireland too. The everything's a grand invention," Brendon confirmed.

"So, Brendon," Ivan said. "Tell me all about the new Duravit self-cleaning toilets."

"I've installed only one, and it was defective. But the replacement seemed to work fine. Are you needing a new toilet?"

"No. It was just a random thought."

"Ah. Well, generally, there's no substitute for elbow grease. Sometimes you just have to bear down on the porcelain to get it really clean."

"Dear God," GoGo said. "My mouth is filled with this miracle of *everything*. Can we discuss something else?"

"Oh, of course, you're so right," Brendon sputtered.

"Relax, Brendon," Ivan said. "I brought it up. Come on, GoGo. Let's get some everything bagels to take home. These kids have barely had a moment alone."

"That was kind, giving us room," Brendon said when they left.

"Yeah, they're pretty great."

"I'm glad you have them."

Many times I've avoided asking questions on the most treacherous of topics. I dare say; I'll go to my death regretting this neglect.

"Brendon?"

"Yes, Peppa?"

"The money. Was it really for your sister?"

"What else would it have been for? Yes. Yes, it was."

"Tell me how it happened."

"Your dad loaned me a small amount. Before I met you."

"But on our first date, you were freaking out about not making enough money. If my dad was already helping, why?" she asked.

"Because I had no idea if it was going to continue. But it did. And after you and I got together, he asked that I not tell you. I didn't feel good about it. But what could I do? He was my boss. And he wanted to help my sister."

"How is she?"

"The drugs have been really tough, but the tumors are reduced," he said. "If they can get them small enough, they'll operate. Nothing is guaranteed, but she has more time now."

"Then, there's hope?"

"Yeah, there's that."

As the bagel shop got busier, both receded into shyness. Peppa stared at the Towers while Brendon stared at their daughter. Occasionally, their eyes would meet and they'd test out smiles. Then Brendon took her hand and laced his fingers through hers. She squeezed hard.

"Did you know that I had no clue what happened to you until recently?" he asked.

"No. I didn't know that."

"Your parents shut me out completely. Your dad dropped me from the work roster. Wouldn't return my calls. I knocked on your door so many times, but no one would answer. Then about a month ago, your dad called out of the blue with a city job lined up for me. That's when he told me about your breakdown. And the pregnancy . . . and Kit's birth. You can't imagine how desperate I've been."

"Is all this really the truth?"

"Why on God's good earth would I lie about such things? I've got nothing left to lose, Peppa."

"Two dozen everything bagels!" GoGo announced, depositing two shopping bags at their feet. "We're set for at least a month."

"Why don't we head out now?" Just as Ivan made the suggestion, Kit began to cry.

"Seems she's got other ideas," Peppa said. "I'm sorry, Ivan."

"No problem. Another fifteen minutes one way or the other won't make a difference," he said.

By now the place was packed, and the decibel level prevented further conversation without raising their voices, so there was nothing to do but wait while Peppa fed Kit. After a few minutes, she became aware of a deep rumble cutting through the din. The noise came from outside, and a man at the next table said it was probably a helicopter that had clearance to fly low. Ivan and GoGo joined the others who'd gathered at the front window, their heads swiveling back and forth, up and down, trying to confirm the source. Then, a collective gasp followed by screams overwhelmed the small shop. Suddenly the sky was engulfed by a massive storm of black dust, and Peppa could no longer see the Towers.

She turned and leaned into Brendon, their child between them. He wrapped his arms around them both. Then, she placed her head close to his ear so that he could hear what she knew, in this precise moment, would likely be the most important words she'd ever say.

"I want to try," she said. "I do. And there are things about me that you need to know."

"I have the rest of my life to listen to you, Peppa."

Dear Virginia, Peppa thought, *we are here. And we're okay.*

END

ACKNOWLEDGMENTS

I am indebted to my publisher, Michelle Halket, for ushering my third novel into the world. Her continued faith in my talent is precisely the kind of miracle a writer needs. Many thanks to my agent Murray Weiss for his wisdom and steady support. Editor Jessica Peirce performed like a magician—intuitive, imaginative, and so very kind. Molly Ringle proofread the final draft with eagle eye precision. And to my publicist, Sheryl Johnston, who put me at ease in an increasingly difficult publishing environment, thank you for placing my book in front of readers, both familiar and new. Dear friends Keren Blankfeld and Zeeva Bukai reviewed drafts, giving essential notes with the insight only fellow authors can. I've been so fortunate for beloved friends like Don Shaw, who provided me with the space to write on an island in the middle of the ocean. And Ellen Levy, whose little house on the mesa in Taos was the refuge I sought to write the bulk of this book. Lastly, I must again acknowledge the late Dr. Howard Welsh, to whom this book is dedicated. With respect and admiration, with gratitude and love. Because without him, Peppa Ryan would likely not exist.

Greetings, Book Lovers,

If you are reading these words, I can reasonably assume that you've read my novel, *Dear Virginia, Wait for Me.* Thank you. And perhaps at this very moment, you've assembled in someone's living room with fellow book club members sipping wine or tea, getting ready to discuss my book. Again, thank you!

This is my third novel, and the one question that is almost always asked of me at public readings or when I attend book clubs is this: Are there parts of me that I've integrated into a character's personality or actions? And, in the case of this book which has a single narrator, is it possible that I am Peppa Ryan? The answer is no, but also, yes. All of my characters, including Peppa, are purely fictional. They emerge from my imagination and in the beginning feel quite foreign. One of the mysteries of writing novels is that by fleshing characters out, little by little and over time, they reveal themselves to me almost like magic. I come to love them, flaws and all, and as if they are real. In the case of Peppa, I don't resemble her in any way, but we do share one thing in common: a fierce determination to escape the deeply limiting conditions of our upbringing. Both Peppa and I are survivors.

Now, here are some questions as starting points for your discussion. Have fun!

With gratitude,

Marcia

There are many themes to consider as we follow Peppa Ryan's path over the course of a year around the time of the Millennium. So much happens to her, the people she loves, and those she comes to love. We witness who she initially believes herself to be, and then discover along with her who she actually is.

1.   First, talk about Peppa Ryan. Her brilliance. Her bravery. Her dreams. Her challenges. And, her choices. In what ways can you relate to this unlikely heroine?

2.   Between 1925 and 1929, Virginia Woolf wrote three seminal novels that examine the interior lives of women. She is now considered the feminist literary icon of her time. Since Virginia is Peppa's advisor and ultimate savior, in what way does Peppa step into empowerment? And is she also a feminist?

3.   Peppa believes she is unattractive and overweight, and she suffers from an actual disorder that causes these notions to feel true for her. Because of these thoughts, she's convinced that she'll never achieve a typical life. Discuss how society sets up women for these feelings of inadequacy, and what has changed since 2001.

4.   One of the leitmotifs in the book is the idea of luck and fate. At times, Peppa strings a series of events together in her mind so that she can then understand the outcome as inevitable. Do you think there is truth in this linear cause and effect? Or do you believe that things happen, for the most part, in a random way?

5.   All of the characters transform in some way. Discuss how Peppa influences, or is unwittingly responsible for, these changes.

6.   The book ends at a pivotal time in our collective history. How do you feel about the ending, and what do you imagine happens to the characters in the next hours?

Photo: Jay Potter

Marcia Butler is the author of a nationally acclaimed memoir and three lauded novels. Prior to becoming an author, Marcia had several creative careers: professional musician, interior designer, and documentary filmmaker. Marcia's writing has been published in *The Washington Post, Literary Hub, PANK Magazine, Psychology Today, Aspen Ideas Magazine, Catapult, Bio-Stories, Kenyon Review,* and others. She was a recipient of a Writer-in-Residence through Aspen Words and the Catto Shaw Foundation and was a writing fellow at the Virginia Center for the Creative Arts. After four decades in New York City, Marcia now calls New Mexico home.